MURDER IN CALISTOGA

A Liz Lucas Cozy Mystery - Book 7

BY

DIANNE HARMAN

Copyright © 2017 Dianne Harman

All rights reserved, including the right to reproduce this book, or portions thereof, in any form without written permission except for the use of brief quotations embodied in critical articles and reviews.

Published by: Dianne Harman
www.dianneharman.com

Interior, cover design and website by
Vivek Rajan

This is a work of fiction. Names, characters, places, and incidents either are the product of the author's imagination or are used fictitiously, and any resemblance to actual persons, living or dead, business establishments, events, or locales, is entirely coincidental.

ISBN: 978-1542733427

CONTENTS

Acknowledgments

Prologue

1	Chapter One	1
2	Chapter Two	5
3	Chapter Three	10
4	Chapter Four	13
5	Chapter Five	16
6	Chapter Six	19
7	Chapter Seven	22
8	Chapter Eight	27
9	Chapter Nine	32
10	Chapter Ten	39
11	Chapter Eleven	43
12	Chapter Twelve	47
13	Chapter Thirteen	51
14	Chapter Fourteen	54
15	Chapter Fifteen	58
16	Chapter Sixteen	63
17	Chapter Seventeen	67
18	Chapter Eighteen	71

19	Chapter Nineteen	74
20	Chapter Twenty	78
21	Chapter Twenty-One	84
22	Chapter Twenty-Two	87
23	Chapter Twenty-Three	91
24	Chapter Twenty-Four	96
25	Chapter Twenty-Five	101
26	Chapter Twenty-Six	108
27	Chapter Twenty-Seven	112
28	Chapter Twenty-Eight	117
29	Chapter Twenty-Nine	121
30	Chapter Thirty	125
31	Recipes	132
32	About Dianne	138

ACKNOWLEDGMENTS

To You, My Readers:

To my readers: Thank you for taking the time to read my books, write reviews, and contact me. I so appreciate your support. Without it, I wouldn't be a bestselling author!

To my family: Mike, Noelle, Michelle, Lamine, Chloe, and Liam. Thank you for your support, your suggestions, and your encouragement. I love you all!

To Vivek: Thank you for your beautiful book covers, handling the technical side of publishing my books, and for your wise counsel!

And lastly, but not leastly, to Tom: Thank you for supporting me on every step of the journey we've shared!

Win FREE Paperbacks every week!

Go to www.dianneharman.com/freepaperback.html and get your FREE copies of Dianne's books and favorite recipes immediately by signing up for her newsletter.

Once you've signed up for her newsletter you're eligible to win three paperbacks. One lucky winner is picked every week. Hurry before the offer ends!

DIANNE HARMAN

PROLOGUE

Nikki Evans stepped out of the hotel and spa building and walked down a short path to a nearby freestanding building that had a sign on the front door which read "Jacuzzi and Sauna." She opened the door and found herself in a small beautifully appointed reception type of room. There was no attendant on duty, but a sign printed in large letters on the reception desk announced that the jacuzzi and sauna facilities were available to hotel/spa guests on a self-service basis.

A door on the right side of the room was labeled "Men's Locker Room" and the door on the left side said "Women's Locker Room." Nikki walked into the women's locker room and exchanged the clothes she was wearing for a fluffy white robe hanging from a clothes rack. She took off her watch and wedding ring, put them in her purse, and placed her purse and street clothes in a metal locker provided for that purpose. The key to the locker was attached to a plastic bracelet and after she locked the locker, she slipped the bracelet with the key attached around her wrist.

A few moments later she opened the doors to the sauna, looking forward to the warm steam heat getting rid of the tension she felt from the never-ending string of arguments she constantly had with Damon, her husband. She didn't know how much longer she could stand the pressure and tension resulting from their tumultuous relationship. It wasn't her fault they had to leave San Francisco when his employer threatened to have him prosecuted for embezzling company funds. She didn't think her friends knew about it, and all she wanted to do while she was here at the spa was forget everything for a few days, while she relaxed, enjoyed herself, and made good use of the fabulous facilities that the spa offered to its guests.

So far, she'd been successful in hiding the fact that Damon had taken a job as a heating and air conditioning installer in Sacramento. The last few years hadn't been easy, and once again she wondered why she even bothered to stay with him. She'd thought Damon would be grateful for the money she'd given him to pay back the company he'd worked for and keep him from going to prison for years. After all, it was her inheritance money that she'd received from her deceased parents. Instead, it only seemed to fuel the anger he directed towards her, as if she was in some way responsible for him having to take a job that was many thousands of dollars below the salary level he was used to being paid when he'd been working in San Francisco.

Nikki shook her head, glad she was away from Damon for the next few days. Even though she hated to admit it, lately she'd become frightened of him. Although he'd never been physically abusive to her, she was pretty sure it was just a matter of time.

And what about me? It's not like the last few years have been a walk in the park for me, she thought as she walked into the sauna and carefully shut the doors. She hung her robe on a wooden wall peg, spread a towel on the redwood bench that stretched the width of the sauna room, and sat down, letting the hot steam seep into her skin and warm her up.

The heat in this sauna is wonderful. It feels like it's melting away the frozen feeling I've had for a long time, ever since Damon told me we had to sell our home in Hillsborough and leave San Francisco. My life was there, my friends, everything, and it was all over within minutes when he came home and told me we had to get out of town yet that afternoon. I'm so looking forward to my time here at the spa. I'm going to do nothing but pamper myself for the next couple of days, and I really need to make a decision about whether I should stay with Damon or leave him. I know I can't go on living my life like this much longer. The heat in this sauna is making me really uncomfortable. I wonder if there's a thermostat in here. It feels like its thirty degrees hotter than it was when I came in a few minutes ago.

She stood up and took her robe from the peg. The heat had become so intense she had trouble catching her breath and she felt dizzy as she walked to the doors. She finally made it to the doors, only to find they were jammed shut and wouldn't open no matter how hard she tried to open them. She frantically screamed out for help and banged on the doors, but to no avail. She tried to force the doors open by throwing her full weight against them, but the doors wouldn't budge.

A sickening feeling swept over her as she realized she was hopelessly trapped in the sauna. Her lungs felt like they were on fire. That was the last conscious thought Nikki Evans had as she collapsed on the floor while the superheated steam kept pouring into the sauna. Fortunately for her, the heat in the sauna was so intense she died within a matter of a few minutes without regaining consciousness.

CHAPTER ONE

Liz and Roger were sitting in the warm sunshine on the patio restaurant of the L'Auberge du Soleil resort located on a ridge high above the Napa Valley. They were enjoying an incredible Mediterranean lunch of goat cheese phyllo stacks with crushed olives, grilled vegetables with a green olive dip and pita chips, and roasted lobster tails with seasoned bread crumbs, which ended with baklava cups. The boxer guard dog Roger had given Liz two years earlier, Winston, was basking in the sun just off the patio. Although the hotel allowed dogs, they had a firm policy that none were allowed in the restaurant, so Roger had looped Winston's leash around a nearby tree while they enjoyed their lunch.

"Roger, would you look at that view?" Liz said. "Being located high on the side of this ridge makes it incredible. On the other side of the highway down below there are vineyards for as far as the eye can see, and this oak-lined canyon makes me feel like I'm in a world all of my own. To think we have today and the rest of the weekend to do nothing but enjoy ourselves. This is such a treat, and what a wonderful anniversary present. Thanks for calling Judy and arranging it."

"Actually, she called me. You know how excited she is about the boutique hotel and spa she bought in Calistoga, and she can't wait for us to see it. It's an older building she's completely remodeled along with adding a number of modern conveniences. I told her we'd do a little wine tasting this afternoon here in the Napa area, and she could plan on us arriving at her hotel in Calistoga around five this evening. I made sure she was okay with us bringing Winston. It worked out great, because I'd been wondering what to do for our anniversary."

"Again, thanks, but I have to tell you I never thought she'd do something like what she's done," Liz said. 'It's a pretty big step for a woman who hasn't worked in thirty years and only then when she got a couple of cameo roles in movies. I knew her three divorce settlements were very generous, but I didn't realize they were that generous."

"Well, I'm sure we're going to hear all about it when we get there. I understand we have the honeymoon suite, and the other five rooms have been rented out by a wealthy woman Judy knows from San Francisco who's hosting a reunion for four friends of hers from college. Judy said they meet every five years, and it was Judy's friend's turn to arrange it this time. Judy told me since this was the first week her hotel was open, she was sure her friend was just trying to throw some business her way, but it was a nice thing to do."

"Roger, you said we were going wine tasting. What wineries did you have in mind?"

"I know it's schmaltzy, but I want to go to the Castello di Amorossa first. That's the one that looks like a castle, and it even has a moat and a drawbridge. After that I want to go to Schramsberg. One of my partners at the law firm in San Francisco told me we shouldn't miss it, because it's got one of the oldest hillside vineyards in Napa. After that, we'll play it by ear. Since you serve wine and appetizers before dinner at the Red Cedar Lodge and Spa, I thought you might like to expand your knowledge, and maybe even buy some wine while we're here."

"Let's get started, but first I need to make a visit to the ladies' room. Be back in five minutes. You might want to give Winston some water while I'm gone. I'll tell the waiter to bring you a soup bowl with water in it." Roger looked at Liz as she walked to the ladies' room. Short auburn hair framed her heart-shaped face and porcelain complexion. Her figure was full-bodied, but he'd never been a fan of thin women. He thought she was even more beautiful now than when he'd first met her at his law office in San Francisco.

As he walked back to the table after giving Winston some water he felt his phone vibrating in his pocket. He took it out and looked at the screen which showed Judy's name and number. "Hi, Judy. We've just finished lunch, and we're getting ready to do some wine tasting, then we'll drive up to your hotel, arriving right around 5:00."

"Roger…" was all Judy could blurt out before she had to stop talking, because she was crying so hard.

"What's wrong, Judy? Are you all right?"

"Yes. No. Oh, Roger, please come now. The police and the coroner are here. It's just horrible."

"Judy, tell me what's happened."

"The woman I told you about, you know my friend Renee from San Francisco."

"Yes, I remember," he said.

"One of the women she brought with her was murdered here at the spa. I can't believe it. She told Renee and the others she wanted to go to the sauna before she even unpacked, because she hadn't had an opportunity to go to one since moving to Sacramento. The others said they wanted to unpack first, and they'd meet her there later. Renee was the first one there and the doors had been jammed shut with some kind of a steel bar. She came to get me, and when we went into the sauna, her friend was slumped over on the floor. She was dead. Roger, please come now."

"We're on our way, Judy. Don't give any statements to the police or the media until I get there. Remember, I'm an attorney. If they ask you anything, tell them your attorney is on his way, and you want to wait until he gets there." He looked at the bill the waiter had brought and put enough cash on the tray to cover it as well as a nice tip. He hurriedly walked over to where he'd secured Winston's leash to a tree and unhooked it.

"Ready, Roger? I am so excited about this," Liz said as she joined them.

"There's been a change of plans," Roger said grimly. "One of the women Judy's friend brought to the spa has been murdered. Judy and the woman found her body in the sauna at Judy's spa. We're going to have to pass on the wine tasting this afternoon. Judy's pretty hysterical, and I'm concerned what she might unwittingly say to the police," he said as they quickly walked to the valet desk to get their car.

"Oh, Roger, the poor thing," Liz said as they headed up the highway towards Calistoga. "To have a murder happen at your spa the first weekend you're open could be the kiss of death for ever making a success of it. I'm sure the media will pick it up, and a brand new business couldn't get any publicity worse than that."

"I agree. Obviously, we have to do everything we can to see that the murderer is found, and the spa's name is cleared. Fortunately, Calistoga is close by, so we should be there in less than half an hour."

CHAPTER TWO

"Hi, Judy. It's Renee. I was cleaning out a desk drawer and found an old photograph from years ago of both of us and our children when they were attending nursery school. It brought back some good memories. How are you and your new boutique hotel and spa doing? Be forewarned, I have an ulterior motive for asking," she said.

"It's coming along great. The hotel is ready to go, and the spa is almost finished. The hotel just needs some painting to make it warm and inviting. I also want to bring in a lot of flowers and plants. You know, things like that.

"The workmen are putting the final touches on the jacuzzi and sauna. It was too expensive to build them as part of the main spa building, so I had a small structure built next to it which contains the jacuzzi and sauna. Since they both had special requirements for heat and water, my contractor decided that was the best way to go. I'm going to open for business on July 28th. My contractor assures me he can finish everything by then. Of course, having the spa and hotel open for business is only the beginning. Now I need to find people to come.

"I've been reluctant to advertise it anywhere, because I was afraid there would be some kind of a snag in the construction schedule, but it looks like it really is going to open on the 28th. I'm so excited I can barely stand it. I'm spending the next two days doing nothing but advertising it on social media sites, updating my web page, and taking out some ads in travel and spa magazines. Who knew I'd become so computer savvy at this age?" she asked laughing. "I guess you really can teach an old dog new tricks."

"You're way ahead of me," Renee responded. "I'm doing well to answer an email, and the thought of having a web page is quite beyond me, which is probably good, because I wouldn't have anything to say on it."

If Judy didn't know Renee so well, she would have thought she was making a tongue-in-cheek statement, but the refreshing thing about Renee, and the thing that never failed to amaze Judy and everyone else, was that Renee was completely oblivious to her beauty and her wealth.

At 5'7" she still looked like the woman Judy had met years ago at the nursery school their children attended. She had a little help from her hairdresser to cover up the grey in her auburn hair these days, but her figure didn't look a bit different than it had then. Everyone in her circle of friends was jealous she'd never even had to visit a plastic surgeon to have a little "work" done. Her complexion was as flawless and as unlined as it had been when they'd first met.

People often commented on how unfair it was that a woman as beautiful as Renee should also be as wealthy as she was. Growing up as an only child, she'd been pampered and adored by her parents who had met an untimely death when she was only twelve years old. They'd been in an automobile accident on their way back to San Francisco after attending a red-carpet movie premiere in Los Angeles. When the pilot of their private plane told them that San Francisco was fogged in and the airport was closed, they'd made the decision to drive home, because they missed their daughter. They'd rented a car and driven north on Highway 101. Unfortunately, it was foggy on the freeway, and they died in an auto accident when a driver making a lane change didn't see their car because of the heavy fog.

Her wealthy parents had willed their considerable estate to Renee. While she was a minor, she was cared for by her uncle who was appointed her guardian and had moved into the family home. When she became twenty-one, the estate her uncle had been holding in trust for her was distributed outright to her. While she was in college at Berkeley, she'd fallen in love with a young man from an equally impressive family. They'd moved into her old family home. Her new husband took over his father's brokerage firm, and his ability to make money for his clients had become legendary in the San Francisco area, surpassed only by his attraction to members of the opposite sex.

The wealth and his irresistibility to women was a combination which took its toll on the marriage. It ended in divorce a few years and two children later, and Renee's uncle, who was a lawyer, made sure that her vast estate was substantially augmented by what she privately thought of as "guilt money" from her ex-husband.

Over the years, she became a well-known patron of the arts in the San Francisco area. While her life seemed to be nothing but a merry-go-round of gallery openings, first nights at whatever event was opening, and having her picture in the San Francisco Chronicle on a weekly basis for attending the parties that mattered to socialite San Franciscans, few people knew that was only a very small part of her life. Her favorite charity that was very close to her heart was the San Francisco Society for Prevention of Cruelty to Animals. Even though it was hardly as glamorous as the opera and the other things she attended, the amount of money she gave to the SPCA kept them solvent.

Every time she visited the facility she promised herself she would not go in the back and look at the dogs. She had three dogs already, and she knew that was enough. Her home in San Francisco was from the "Painted Ladies" era of Victorian and Edwardian houses that had been painted in three or more pastel colors which accentuated their architectural details. They were highly desirable homes, and hers was one of the most beautiful.

Although her home was large and had been in her family for several generations, the back yard was small. She limited her dogs to a miniature schnauzer, a toy poodle, and mixture of who knew what – a result of the one time she'd allowed herself to go to the kennels in the back of the SPCA facility.

Renee had many friends, but her friends from when they had been roommates in college were still the most important to her. Every five years, no matter where any of them were living, she and four of them got together somewhere in the world. The last reunion had taken place in Provence, France, because Nancy's husband had been transferred to Paris to manage a large international company's office which was headquartered in Paris. Whichever roommate's turn it was to host the reunion got to choose where they met. The reunion five years earlier had been Nancy's turn, and so they'd traveled to Provence.

This year it was Renee's turn, and she'd decided to have the other four fly to San Francisco, stay at her home for one night, and then have her driver drive them to Calistoga for three days of shopping, wine-tasting, and spa treatments. She'd originally thought she'd treat them to the luxurious Meadowood Spa in Napa, but when she found out Judy was opening a boutique hotel and spa, she decided instead to support her by holding the reunion there.

"Judy, that date, July 28th, is just perfect," Renee said. "I want to reserve five rooms for me and my friends. You may remember I told you some time ago that I was in charge of the reunion this summer, and this will be perfect, plus you can advertise you're already booked for the first weekend that you're open for business. That should be impressive to some people. Can you do that?"

"Oh, Renee, that's wonderful. I don't think you've ever met my friend Liz and her husband, Roger. We met when she lived in San Francisco. Actually, she's probably the reason I bought the hotel and spa. She has a lodge and spa in Red Cedar about an hour north of San Francisco. I've been there several times, and I always thought owning a hotel and spa would be something I'd like to do. Actually, it's been getting higher and higher on my bucket list, and when I saw that a small hotel was for sale when I was here in Calistoga on a vacation, it seemed like fate.

"Anyway, they're coming here that weekend, too, and since the hotel has six rooms, it works beautifully. You and your friends will take five of the rooms, and Liz and Roger will take the sixth room, which is actually the honeymoon suite. We serve breakfast, and I found a woman who's a superb cook. I decided not to hire a chef for nightly dinners, because there are so many great restaurants in Calistoga. Do you need anything special for your guests? Do you know if any of them have allergies or things like that?"

"Not that I know about, at least none of them have ever mentioned any. I'll send you a deposit to hold the rooms. You have my email, so you can send me the address and directions. I think you'll like my friends. It doesn't seem possible, but we've been good friends since we were in college."

"If you have a minute, why don't you tell me something about them?"

"Sure, that's probably a good idea. Judy, let me call you back. I'm expecting a delivery, and it looks like it's here. It'll be just a couple of minutes."

CHAPTER THREE

Here we go again, Amber Ruiz thought. *It's not as if I have nothing better to spend my money on than go to San Francisco, be picked up by Renee's chauffeur-driven limousine, pretend I'm enjoying the evening at Renee's spectacular home, and hope nobody finds out just how poor my husband and I really are. Then we're going to some fancy schmancy spa and boutique hotel in Calistoga where I'll probably have to spend money on something I can't afford, so I won't look needy.*

I probably should just admit to them that I can't afford to go on a trip like this, even if Renee is footing the bill for everything but the airfare. I also probably should drive there instead of flying, but everyone will want to know why I didn't fly, and I don't want to admit I really can't afford a plane ticket. Daniel is so supportive and always urges me to go on these trips, but I know how tight things are. With the drought the last couple of years, it's even harder to make a living from farming, plus a lot of the workers we've used in the past have gone back to Mexico. They were afraid they'd be deported because they were here illegally, and I can't blame them.

I've never told Daniel about the conversation I overheard between Renee and Nikki when we were in college. He's such a good man, he'd tell me to forget it, that it was only words said when someone was young, and I need to let it go, but I can't. If I decided to no longer attend the reunions, I'd probably have to tell Renee that not only can I not afford them, I can't stand to be with Nikki.

I wish I could get over this anger I still feel for her. I know it's not healthy for me, and it's stupid because it's been so many years, but every time I think about it, I get mad all over again, particularly when reunion time rolls around. I'll never forget it, and I remember it just like it happened yesterday, and I have to admit I hate her as much today as I hated her the day it all happened.

My class was cancelled, and I let myself into the apartment the five of us were sharing. I heard voices and realized Renee and Nikki were having an argument, well kind of an argument, because Renee really never raised her voice or got angry about anything. Honestly, that woman is too good to be true. For some reason, rather than let them know I'd returned, I listened, and to this day I regret it.

"Honestly, Renee, we could get anyone to live with us. We don't need to be saddled with someone who barely knows how to use a knife and fork. I'd be willing to bet this apartment is a whole lot better than the house Amber grew up in down in the Central Valley. I know she's on a scholarship and smart, but I think your putting up with her is almost like giving money to a homeless person. I've seen you do that before, and this isn't a whole lot different. You probably think you're doing her a favor, but she might begin to think she's as good as we are, and that wouldn't be fair. She's a real nobody and never will be a somebody. It's a total waste of our time to be around her."

"Nikki, I can't believe what you're saying. Amber is a wonderful person. She's smart and giving, and she's been a wonderful roommate. I don't know why you're objecting to her."

"I'll tell you why. That guy she sees, Daniel Ruiz, should have stayed in Mexico. Just like her, he's a nothing, and I'm embarrassed when people see him coming here to our apartment. I mean, think about it. The people we grew up with and our friends are so far above Amber and Daniel. Really, Renee, admit it, they're both nobodies and a couple of big time losers."

"That's a cruel thing to say, Nikki, and beneath you. I consider this conversation to be closed."

Amber backed out the front door, silently closed it, then opened it, and called out, "Hi everyone, my class was cancelled, so I'm back early."

"Hi, Amber, I'm just on my way to class. You're lucky yours was cancelled. Considering that I haven't really studied for mine, I wish it was mine that had been cancelled," Nikki said brightly, gathering up her book bag, and waving to them as she walked out the front door.

What a two-faced person she is. Someday something bad is going to happen to her, and I won't shed a tear over it. In fact, when she dies I'll dance on her grave.

Twenty-five years is a long time to wait for revenge, but as Don Corleone said in the Godfather movie, "It is a dish that tastes best when it is cold."

CHAPTER FOUR

"Sorry for the interruption, Judy. That was the company that's going to reupholster my couch. One of my dogs, I think it was Lucy, the schnauzer, decided that my suede couch looked very inviting, and it was even more inviting when she could pull the stuffing out of the pillows. I know it seems silly to keep the old couch. Actually, I'd probably be better off if I just got a new one, but I remember Mom and Dad sitting on it in the evening after Dad got home from work, and I have sentimental feelings about it."

"I understand. I have a couple of things like that, and my children can't understand why I bother to keep them. It's an emotional thing. I can't bring myself to let go of them."

"That's it exactly. Anyway, back to my friends. I want to tell you a little about each of them. I told you about when I went to Provence five years ago for the reunion, and what a great excuse it was to go to Provence. I'm kind of sorry Nancy still isn't there, because I could sure redo that trip."

"Yes, I remember. Actually, I was very jealous. Paris is something that's always been on list of places I want to go, and now with the spa and hotel, I have no idea when I'll ever get there. Where does Nancy live now?"

"Her husband was transferred to their Los Angeles office, so she's not that far away, but it's kind of funny. Even though she's only a short plane ride away, we only see each other at these reunions. It seems strange now that I think about it, but that's how we do it."

"I think it's nice you have friends you care enough about that you want to get together with them every few years."

"Yes, it is. The next one I want to tell you about is Nikki Evans. I'm not real sure what's going on with her."

"What do you mean?"

"Well, her husband was a very wealthy real estate developer in San Francisco, but something happened to him a few years ago and they left the San Francisco area. She's never talked about it. Now they live in Sacramento, and I don't know what he's doing, if anything. I know she works in some state Senator's office, but I don't think it's a very good job, and I don't think she makes much money. Quite frankly, I'm always surprised she's able to attend our reunions. Her clothes look like they came from Goodwill, and her hair is kind of a dishwater grey. On some women grey hair looks great, but with her I think it's because she can't afford to go to a hairdresser."

"I'm surprised the San Francisco rumor mill didn't give you some hints about what happened."

"So am I, but I never heard anything. I feel sorry for her. She's a proud woman, and I don't think she wants us to know what, if anything, her husband is doing. I've heard there have been some marital problems, but since that happens in almost every marriage, I haven't paid much attention to them."

"After three marriages, I can certainly attest to that," Judy said wryly.

"The next friend I want to tell you about is Tiffany Jones. She's a very interesting person. Several years ago, her husband died of a heart attack. He was only fifty-four at the time, so it came as quite a shock to everyone. They lived in Seattle, and Tiffany was the vice-president of a large clothing chain that's headquartered there.

"Unfortunately, only a few months after his death, she was let go from the company. There was a lot of speculation they got rid of her because of her age. It seemed a little too convenient that a woman in her thirties, who hadn't been with the company for very long, took over Tiffany's job. She was devastated, but then a few months later, she was approached by the main competitor of the company she'd previously worked for to go to work for them. Long story short, she's now the vice-president of that company and doing better than she ever did while working for the first one. It's kind of a 'warm your heart' story."

"Those are the things all of us who are aging need to hear," Judy said. "So often we're made to feel like it's all over when we hit fifty, and it's not. Tiffany's a case in point. I believe you said you had four friends in your reunion group. Who's the last one?"

"Her name is Amber Ruiz. She came from a very poor family in the Central Valley. She told us once her parents were sharecroppers. She went to Berkeley on a scholarship, and even though she's quite intelligent, she's never done much with her life. She married a farmer from Salinas. I think he's what might be called a 'truck farmer'. Although she comes to the reunions, I've always felt there's some jealousy there. For some reason, she seems particularly resentful of Nikki, but I don't know why. That's pretty much a thumbnail sketch of who will be with me when we arrive at your hotel on the 28th. I better go. Tonight's opening night at the opera, and I sit on the Board of Directors. Send me the address of your hotel, and I'll mail you a deposit. Judy, I'm really looking forward to our stay at your hotel and spa."

"I will, and I'll also send you a list of the spa services that are available. Why don't you choose some for your guests, and I'll make sure their experiences are memorable. As I said earlier, we have a jacuzzi and a sauna, so tell them to bring a bathing suit, if they wish, although that's optional. Again, Renee, thanks!"

CHAPTER FIVE

Simone picked up the Calistoga News and couldn't believe the headline which read "Boutique Spa and Hotel Opening July 28th". She put the paper down and took a sip of her coffee. So much for her source that had told her the Calistoga Planning Commission was going to deny the requested variances needed to build a jacuzzi and sauna building on the property. Denial of the requested variance would have effectively blocked the owner from opening a hotel and spa due to the lack of jacuzzi and sauna.

The next time Jim Michaelson runs for City Council, he better not ask me for a dime. Matter of fact, think I'll give him a call and tell him that.

She pulled his name up on her cell phone and tapped on the phone icon. A moment later a voice said, "Hi, Simone. How are you?"

"Not well, Jim, not well at all. Have you looked at the Calistoga News this morning?" she asked.

"No. There's a City Council meeting tonight, and I've been reading the agenda to get ready for it. Why?"

"Do you recall a few months ago when I gave a maximum contribution to your campaign for City Council, and I had three members of my staff do the same?"

"Of course, I do. I'm sure that was one of the reasons I won the election. How do you think I could forget something like that?"

"From what the paper says, it's rather obvious you did forget something, like talking to the person you appointed to the Calistoga Planning Commission to make sure that no jacuzzi or sauna was built on the property of the hotel and spa that Judy Rasmussen is refurbishing. That's what you forget. According to the paper, it's supposed to open the end of July."

It was quiet on the other end of the phone for several long moments, then Jim began to speak. "Simone, I am so sorry. I told Henry I wanted to make sure his approval was never given for the sauna and jacuzzi to be built. I can't understand what happened, but I'll call him right now and find out. Anyway, everybody knows you've got the most elegant and best spa in town. It's probably too late to do anything about it now, and really, it doesn't matter. With the following you have, that new hotel and spa will probably be out of business in weeks…"

Simone cut him off in mid-sentence and said, "Don't try and weasel out of this, Jim. I'd be willing to bet you're lying through your teeth, and you never told Henry to make sure it was prevented. You've been so busy telling everyone how important you are now that you're on the Calistoga City Council, I'm sure it slipped through the cracks.

"I'd like to make one thing quite clear, Jim, as of this moment any future requests from you for money from me will slip through the cracks as well. This is a small town, and it doesn't take much money to get elected to public office here in Calistoga. I'm sure your next opponent will welcome contributions from me and some of my staff, and you can go back to being a used car salesman." She pressed end call on her phone and threw the phone across the room where it hit a mirror and shattered it.

Swell, that's all I need. A broken mirror means seven years of bad luck. Looks like it's already starting with that Rasmussen woman's place set to open on July 28th. Well, since I can't do anything about it, I better think of something

I can do to make sure she gets a lot of bad publicity and never makes a go of it.

Simone took another sip of her coffee as a smile began to spread across her face. *I wonder how much bad publicity the spa would get if a death took place there just after it opened.* She stood up and opened the door to the hallway. Her cleaning lady, Josie, was in the living room doing her weekly dusting.

"Josie, I'm sorry to bother you, but would you mind coming in here for a moment? I'd like you to make a call for me." Josie walked into the room, an inquisitive look on her face.

"I'd like you to call this number and ask if they have any available reservations for the weekend of July 28th. If the person answering the phone says they do, hang up. If she says they don't, thank her and hang up. Really, it's very simple. Understand?"

"Yes," she said, looking oddly at Simone. Josie placed the call and when she was finished Josie turned to her and said, "The hotel is booked that weekend. Evidently a woman from San Francisco is bringing a group of friends for a reunion they have every five years, and she wanted to have it at the hotel because the owner is a friend of hers."

"That's all I need, Josie. You can go back to work. Thanks."

Simone sat down at her computer to see if she could find the information that she needed to implement her plan.

CHAPTER SIX

"Nikki, are you really thinking about going to that reunion this year?" Damon Evans asked his wife.

"Of course I am, and I wouldn't miss it for anything. We're meeting at Renee's home in San Francisco, and the next day she's treating us to a couple of days at a new spa some friend of hers is opening in Calistoga. Since it's the only time I get to do something just for me, I'm really looking forward to it. You got all the money my parents left me, so I figure I at least deserve something once every five years. I don't have much else to get excited about anymore."

"Can't let a day go by without reminding me what a loser I am, can you, Nikki? Think I'm having a good time installing people's furnaces and air conditioning units like I did when I was putting myself through college? Think I like living in this crummy apartment on the wrong side of Sacramento?" he asked, pounding his fist on the table. "I hate every minute of what my miserable life's become."

"Not like it's my fault, Damon. I wasn't the one who got caught with my hand in the cookie jar. Oh no, that was my smarter-than-everyone husband. Unfortunately, the bookkeeper at the real estate development company was even smarter than you, because she's the one that uncovered your embezzlement scheme. You're just lucky you didn't go to jail. Look at the bright side. We live so close to Nic's

Bar you can roll home on the nights you can't walk."

"Maybe I should have gone to jail, and then maybe I'd be rid of you nagging me every day of my life. So, what do you tell those hoity-toity friends of yours when you see them at these reunions? Do you tell them you're working for some Senator in his back office, while all the lookers and younger women are working in the front office? Think those friends, as you call them, ever wonder why you've let yourself go, and you look like an old woman?" he taunted.

"I don't want them to find out about you, because they'll wonder why I stayed with you. We never talk about it, but I'll bet everybody knows you left San Francisco with your tail between your legs. That's no mystery, but the real mystery is why I even stay with you."

"No mystery, Nikki. You and I both know why. You're just still grateful I married you when you found out you were pregnant. Too bad you lost the kid, but since you did, none of your fancy friends ever had to know about it. They just thought we got married out of love. Right, like we both had stars in our eyes.

"Over the years, I've thought about it a lot, and I'm pretty sure the timing wasn't right for the kid to have been mine. I was just the young and dumb college guy who felt he needed to do the right thing and marry you. Believe me, that was one of the worst decisions I've ever made. If I'd been smarter, I'd be a free man and not have you hanging around my neck like a millstone."

"How can you even say something like that? Without my parents' money, you would have gone to prison. You may have been free from being a married man, but you'd be wearing an orange prison suit on your body instead of a millstone around your neck. In many ways, it was the best decision you ever made," she said crying and throwing her napkin down on the table. She stormed into the bedroom and threw herself on the bed, sobbing.

A moment later, she heard Damon say, "Who knows, Nikki? Maybe something bad will happen to you on your trip, and I'll be a free man. Might be the best thing for both of us." He slammed the bedroom door and then she heard him slam the front door as he left the house.

A spa in Calistoga, hmm… That means it'll have a jacuzzi and a sauna. Lots of things could go wrong with the temperature controls in either one of those places, and it's not very far from here, Damon thought on his way to his favorite watering hole, the neighborhood bar two streets over. *Be a shame if something happened to Nikki, then again, my life would be a lot easier without her around.*

CHAPTER SEVEN

"Mac, did you see in the Calistoga News this morning where that spa and hotel on the property next to ours is going to open for business on July 28th? Guess the owner named it Serenity Hotel and Spa. How much of a cliché is that? Anyway, I thought you were going to talk to the new owner and see if we could buy it from her. We could sure use the five acres it sits on."

"Winnie, I've tried to buy that property from her more times than I've told you. I tried to buy it several times when it went up for sale, but the old owner and this Judy Rasmussen cut a deal, and I was shut out. Old lady Jackson never did like us, so I figure she sold it to her out of spite. Believe me, I want that acreage to grow more grapes on as badly as you do. The old lady had three acres on the far side planted with grapes. I looked the other day, and the vines are still there. Guess this Rasmussen woman plans to operate the spa and hotel plus do what old lady Jackson did, sell the grapes."

"There must be some way for us to get our hands on that property, Mac. Our vineyard is fully planted, so acquiring more acreage is the only way we can grow our business. If we could get that property, we could raze the spa and the hotel, and then we'd have five more acres for our vines. The other vineyards that back up to our property aren't going to sell their property to us. We've got to figure out some way to make it happen."

"Winnie, I don't know how far you're willing to go to get that property, but I've got a couple of ideas in mind."

"At this point, I'd be willing to try anything. For the last three years, we've run out of wine because we can't grow enough grapes. Your success over the years as a vintner, plus your cousin's knowledge, has resulted in wine connoisseurs placing their orders with us before we even have the annual crush. You and your cousin have done a fabulous job, but there's no way we can increase our income without an increase in the supply of grapes we need to make the wine. We could charge more for the wine, but ours is already the most expensive wine in the valley. I really don't think we can do that."

"Well," Mac said, "several things come to mind. I can try to buy the property one more time before she officially opens. The problem with that is she's put a lot of money into the new building that houses the jacuzzi and sauna, not to mention renovating the hotel and spa. If she did sell it, I imagine she'd put a very hefty price on it, and it would take us years to make enough money from the increased sales in wine to break even and start making a profit. Let's face it. Since we're already in our fifties, realistically we would be in our late seventies or so before we'd turn a profit. That doesn't sound like a very good plan to me."

"I agree. I think we can forget that idea. I was thinking about a fire. It would destroy the hotel and the spa and even with insurance, there's a good chance she wouldn't want to spend the time, money, and energy to rebuild it."

"Yeah, that's an idea, Winnie, but it's got some serious drawbacks."

"Like what?"

"Like what if it got out of hand and destroyed our vineyards, to say nothing of the house, the presses, wine tasting room, and everything else of ours? It would present a potential danger not only to us but to the other winemakers in the area, too. If it was ever discovered that we were the cause of the fire, and it destroyed a lot of other places, we'd probably be lynched before we ever went to trial and prison. I don't like that option."

"Well, we have to do something. Got any other ideas?"

"As a matter of fact, I do. What if a death occurred at her spa on the opening weekend? If that happened the Rasmussen woman and her spa would get a boatload of bad publicity which would probably result in nobody wanting to go there. A few months of no money coming in might make this Rasmussen woman very amenable to selling at a far more reasonable price than what she would probably get if she sold today."

"Mac, you told me all of the things that could go wrong with a fire, but if we, or either one of us, was convicted of murder, prison would practically be guaranteed."

"Usually I'd agree with you, but what if someone died in the sauna?"

"Why in there?" Winnie asked.

"Because I've spent a lot of time looking through a telescope while they were building the jacuzzi and sauna building, and for some reason the temperature controls are on the outside of the building, not inside. I suppose they installed the controls in that location so the owner or her employees can check to make sure the heat to the sauna is turned off after the building closes for the night and the front door is locked."

"Are you saying a murder could occur in the sauna or the jacuzzi?"

"Exactly, and I think it would be impossible to find out who did it if it's done right."

"So exactly how do you think this murder could be committed in such a way that it would be impossible to catch the perpetrator?"

Winnie asked.

"Like I just told you, the temperature controls for the sauna are located on the outside of the building near the front door. I saw the workmen install it there when I was watching them with my telescope. Anyone can access those controls by simply opening the control box, which by the way, does not have a lock on it.

"It would be a rather simple matter to wait until someone is in the sauna and then sneak into the building and put some kind of a brace against the sauna doors, so the person inside the sauna couldn't open them. Then, on the way out, stop at the temperature control box and turn the dial up to the maximum strength heat. At that setting the temperature in the sauna could probably go as high as 140 degrees, and the person would die of heat stroke in a matter of a few minutes."

"What would you use as a brace to prevent the doors to the sauna from being opened?"

"I don't know. I suppose it could be almost anything that would jam the doors tightly shut and prevent them from being opened. Maybe a piece of lumber, a metal bar, even a strong sturdy chair could be wedged up against the doors in such a way as to make it impossible to open the sauna doors from the inside."

"If a murder occurred that way, are you thinking it would be one of her guests?"

"Yes," Mac said, "I guess it's going to be a case of being in the wrong place at the wrong time. I think we'd be better off not knowing who it is."

"I agree. You really think something like this would work?"

"I not only think it would work, I think it's going to have to work if we want that property, and I believe both of us are fully committed to getting it, even if it has to be done that way. Are you on board?" Mac asked, looking at her intently.

Winnie thought for a moment and said, "Yes. I don't like it, but I don't see that we have any other choice."

"Unfortunately, Winnie, we don't."

CHAPTER EIGHT

"There it is, Roger, the Serenity Hotel and Spa. It's really beautiful. What a horrible thing for Judy to have happen on her opening weekend."

"Couldn't agree more. Looks like the police, paramedics, and the coroner are already here. Okay, get ready to give Judy some moral support," he said as he opened his car door.

Judy met them at the door, crying softly. She gave each of them a hug and said, "I'm so glad you're here. This is the worst thing that's ever happened to me. Renee is blaming herself for bringing her friends here, and I think they're all in shock. Come in."

They followed her down the hall to a large room where everyone had gathered. Judy introduced Roger and Liz to Renee and her friends. Roger walked over to where the chief of police was standing and said, "I'm Roger Langley, Mrs. Rasmussen's attorney. What's going on?"

"I'm Chief Jerry Oliphant, it's nice to meet you," he said, extending his hand.

Roger looked at him for a moment and then said, "You bear a strong resemblance to a law partner of mine by the name of Jake Oliphant and with that unusual last name, I'm wondering if you're related."

"We certainly are. Jake's my brother."

"Of course, now that I think about it he did mention to me once that his brother lived in the Napa Valley and was the chief of police of some town in the area. Small world."

"That it is, and quite frankly, this couldn't have happened at a worse time. We're overloaded with tourists that are here this time of year, and there have been two other murders in the valley recently, plus I'm scheduled to meet Jerry and the rest of the extended family for a reunion in Yosemite tomorrow.

"My deputies are overworked as it is. I was reluctant to take the time off for the reunion, but it's the first time the whole family has ever been able to get together. Since they're coming from all over the United States, my wife and everyone else would never forgive me for missing it, plus several of them have already left for it, because they're driving. That's not to even mention what my in-laws would think of me if I missed it. It's a second marriage for both of us, and I think they still have some doubts about the man their daughter married. They really liked my wife's first husband."

"This is going to sound pretty off the wall, Chief, but my wife, Liz, she's the woman over there who's talking to Mrs. Rasmussen, has been involved in investigating a number of murder cases. I have no idea how she seems to get involved, but she does. Anyway, she's helped solve several of them. I imagine it kind of goes against your policy to have a non-law enforcement person help you, but since Mrs. Rasmussen is such a good friend of hers, I'm sure Liz will be getting involved whether you stay in town or not."

"Roger, are you suggesting I go to Yosemite as planned and see what your wife can find out while I'm away?"

"That's exactly what I'm suggesting. Although I'll be here for the next couple of days, I have to return to Red Cedar Sunday afternoon, but I'm sure Liz could stay until you return. It might make your life a little easier, and, as it turns out, she really is quite good at this. Let me introduce you to her."

Roger and the chief walked over to where Liz and Judy were talking and Roger said, "Liz, I want to introduce you to the chief of police, Jerry Oliphant. It turns out he's Jake Oliphant's brother. He's one of the partners at the law firm in San Francisco, and I think he even joined us for dinner one night when there was a late business meeting."

"Yes, I remember Jake. It's nice to meet you, Chief, although I wish it was under different circumstances."

"Mrs. Langley, this is going to sound rather strange, but your husband tells me you've been involved in solving several murders. Is that true?"

She looked over at Roger and then back at the chief. "Yes, why do you ask?"

"I'll be honest. There's never a good time for a murder, but this one comes at a particularly bad time for me. My department is already overloaded with work, and I am leaving early tomorrow afternoon for a three-day family reunion in Yosemite. Members of my family are coming from all over the United States, and while I feel I should be here to help with this case, my personal life would be a disaster if I missed the reunion."

"I can certainly understand that. Is there something I can do to help you, Chief?"

"Under ordinary circumstances, no, but these are extraordinary circumstances. Roger tells me you'll probably be getting involved in this case anyway, as you told him you want to help Mrs. Rasmussen. I imagine you might find out a bit more than I'm going to be told by either her or Mrs. Simmons. Any information they give you might help me solve the case when I get back. I've found people often tell law enforcement personnel just the basic facts of what they saw when they discovered the body and choose to hold back any unverified facts or suspicions they might have. I'm thinking you might be better able to find out some of those unverified facts or suspicions better than I can.

"I guess what I'm suggesting is that I talk to Mrs. Rasmussen and Mrs. Simmons regarding the discovery of Mrs. Evans' body. Tonight, maybe you could talk to both of them in a little more depth, and see if you can find out any additional information. I'd like to talk to you tomorrow morning before I leave, and based on what they tell you tonight, we might be able to come up with some things you could do as legwork for me while I'm gone. Normally, I wouldn't consider anything like this, but I'm afraid I don't have a choice. Naturally, I can't force you to do this. It would strictly be on a voluntary basis.

"Based on what you find out, we might come up with some things you could do to help me, because the immediate time right after a murder is usually crucial to solving it. We'd share our information. I'd call you every evening to see what, if anything, you've found out that day. I've never done anything like this with someone who isn't in law enforcement, but sometimes things in life call on you to try a new method. I'd like you to be the new method. What do you think?"

"Chief, I'd be happy to help you if I can. If we could share our information, that would be a big help, because I'd feel like I was doing something to help Judy find out who the murderer is," Liz said.

"Since I'll be out of town, I probably won't have much information to share, but I will be checking in with my department on a daily basis, and of course they'll have a phone number where I can be reached, so if they get a lead or someone calls something in, I'll certainly share that with you."

"I'm happy to do what I can."

"Okay, let's do it," the chief said. "Right now, I want to take a statement from each of them. Roger, since you're Mrs. Rasmussen's attorney, and your wife is a friend of hers, I'm sure she won't mind if your wife sits in on the conversation. I'll talk to her first, and then I want to talk to Mrs. Simmons. The other three women who came with her were evidently still in their rooms when the murder was discovered. Naturally, I'll ask them if they know anything, but based on what I've briefly been told, I doubt if they do."

CHAPTER NINE

"Ladies," Chief Oliphant said, "I'm going to take each of you into another room one at a time and take your statements. I know it seems silly, but it's kind of a prerequisite for people in law enforcement to interview witnesses separately rather than in a group. Roger Langley is Mrs. Rasmussen's attorney, and at my request, I've asked Roger's wife, Liz Langley, to join us as well. Do any of you have any objections to this method?"

They all shook their heads from side to side indicating no, they were fine with Roger and Liz being present when their statements were taken. The chief looked at Judy and said, "Mrs. Rasmussen, let's begin with you. Which room would you like us to use?"

"The dining room would probably be the best. Naturally there's a large table in there, and you can spread out papers if you need to." The four of them walked into the dining and sat down at the table.

"All right, Mrs. Rasmussen, would you tell me exactly what happened from the time Renee Simmons and her group came to the hotel and spa until you discovered the body?"

"Yes. They arrived about two this afternoon. They drove here in Renee's limousine, and after her driver had brought their luggage inside, he left and from what I overheard he and Renee saying, he went to visit his sister down in St. Helena. Renee told him she'd call him about a half an hour before they would be ready to go out to dinner this evening."

"When the guests were all inside the hotel, what happened?"

"Renee introduced me to everyone, because even though Renee and I've been friends for many years, I'd never met any of the others. After that, I gave each of them a key to their room. Nikki, the woman who died, said she wanted to go directly to the sauna before she unpacked. She said she wanted to let the steam help her get rid of the stress she'd been under recently. Renee told her she'd join her, but she wanted to unpack first. The others said they wanted to unpack as well, and they went upstairs to their rooms."

"Did Nikki Evans go to the sauna?"

"Yes. I pointed the building out to her, and the last time I saw her alive she was walking down the path towards it."

"Did she change clothes before she left?"

"No," Judy said. "I told her we keep towels and robes in the women's locker room, and she could help herself. She said she'd unpack and change clothes when she returned from the sauna."

"Did you accompany her to the sauna?"

"No, as I said, I pointed it out to her, and she walked there alone. I went back to my office and did some paperwork. The next thing I knew Renee was knocking on the office door. She said there was a heavy metal bar inserted through both handles of the doors to the sauna, and she didn't know if she should take it out. She couldn't figure out why someone would put it there. Renee and I walked over to the sauna." Judy stopped and took a sip of water from the glass sitting on the table in front of her.

"Take your time, Mrs. Rasmussen. I'm sure this is not easy for you."

Judy looked at him and said, "No, this is horrible. I've never been involved in anything like this. Anyway, when we got to the sauna I saw that Renee had been right. Some type of a metal bar had been attached to the door handles preventing the doors from being opened from the inside. I was able to remove the metal bar, and then I opened the sauna doors, but we couldn't go in for a few moments because it was so hot in the sauna.

"When I decided to have a sauna and jacuzzi here at the spa, I did a lot of research on them. I knew they could be dangerous for certain people. One of the things I read said that people with various skin diseases, high blood pressure, and other health issues should not be in temperatures over ninety degrees Fahrenheit. I thought that was a good rule of thumb."

"Since you just opened your hotel and spa, had you tested the temperature controls beforehand, and when did you turn the heat on in anticipation of the guests coming for this weekend?"

"The company that installed them had a series of checks they did on the sauna as well as the jacuzzi, one of them being to check the temperature levels multiple times to ensure that the temperature controls worked properly and were safe. They did that for several days. Turning it off, bringing it back up, turning it off, again and again. I had turned the sauna control to 90 degrees this morning. I felt that would give it plenty of time to get to the proper temperature. I have no idea how it got so hot in there."

"I can tell you, Mrs. Rasmussen. As you know, the controls are on the outside of the building, and one of my men noticed that it had been set to 140 degrees. That temperature is high enough that it would easily result in death for almost anyone who stayed in the sauna for more than just a few minutes. Do you have any idea who could have tampered with the temperature controls?"

Roger interrupted their conversation and said, "Judy, that calls for your opinion, and you don't have to answer that." He looked at the chief and said, "Sorry, but most of my background has been in criminal defense, and I think that's a question better addressed at another time."

"No, Roger, I'd like to answer it," Judy said. "Chief Oliphant, I don't have any idea why it would have been turned that high or who could have possibly done it. Absolutely none."

"All right. When you did walk into the sauna what did you find?"

"I opened the doors with Renee next to me, and when we walked in, we saw Nikki Evans. She was nude laying on the upper level of the benches in the sauna near the door."

"Did you or Mrs. Simmons touch anything?"

"No, we were both in shock. I did touch the doors to open them, but that's it."

"What did you do then, Mrs. Rasmussen?"

"I think we both stood there for a moment in shock. We knew there was nothing we could do to help poor Nikki, since it was obvious she was dead. I remember pulling Renee's arm and telling her we needed to call the police. We returned to the hotel, went to my office, and I called the police. You were here in just a few minutes. The paramedics were called by one of your policemen. When they determined that Nikki was in fact dead, the paramedics called the coroner and after he examined her, he took her body to the morgue."

"Yes, that's standard operating procedure. Had the other guests come downstairs by the time you returned to the hotel?"

"No, I think they heard the sirens, and that's when they came downstairs."

"Did you or Renee Simmons tell them what had happened to Nikki Evans?"

"One of them, I don't remember which one, noticed that Renee was shaking and pale. She asked what had happened. Renee told them what we'd discovered and that Nikki was dead. About that time the police and paramedics had entered the hotel lobby, and I told them that Nikki Evans' body was in the building with the words 'Jacuzzi and Sauna' written on it."

"Is there anything else you can think of that might be relevant to her murder?"

"Yes, there is one more thing that I think you should know. I told you when Renee and I went to the sauna, I found a heavy metal bar that was holding the doors to the sauna shut. Because of the requirement to provide handicapped access to the sauna, it has a double door type of entry with an exterior grab handle on each door. The double doors allow a person confined to a wheelchair to easily enter the sauna. The metal bar was wedged between the two outside door handles and effectively jammed the doors shut so they couldn't be opened from inside the sauna. The metal bar was about eighteen inches long and appeared to be a piece of steel rebar, like the kind that's used in construction projects.

"Keep in mind, Chief, that the construction of my jacuzzi and sauna building was completed only two days before I was scheduled to open for business on the 28th, today. The contractor hasn't hauled away some of the leftover scrap construction materials from the job site, which I'd earlier noticed included several small pieces of steel rebar. I can't say for sure, but my guess is the steel rebar that was used to jam shut the doors to the sauna came from that leftover pile of construction materials."

"Thanks for that bit of information, Mrs. Rasmussen. I was wondering where that steel bar might have come from, and that explains it. We'll be sure to check the piece of rebar that was jammed in the door handles for fingerprints. We might just get lucky and find a good set of prints.

"By the way, I'm going to be treating the death of Nikki Evans as a homicide based on the fact that the doors to the sauna were effectively locked by jamming the steel rebar in the door handles and then turning up the temperature control to 140 degrees. The poor woman never had a chance to get out alive. I don't have any more questions for you. Is there anything else you would like to add to your statement that might help us catch the murderer?"

Judy was quiet for several moments and appeared to be in deep thought. Liz knew Judy very well. They'd traveled together and been very close friends for years. She knew Judy was holding something back from the police chief and made a mental note to ask her what it was when he was gone.

"Chief, I've told you everything I know. This was a woman I met only a few minutes before she died. There's simply nothing more I can add to what I've already told you."

"Okay, that wraps it up as far as any more questions I have for you. It's Friday afternoon, and it may be difficult to get the sauna serviced over the weekend, but I strongly recommend you consider putting some sort of a lock on that temperature control box. It's sort of like an accident waiting to happen, although I rather doubt any of your guests will want to go into the sauna this weekend."

Judy wryly laughed. "Let's be honest. When word of Nikki's death gets out, I may never have another guest at the hotel and spa. I not only feel terrible about Nikki dying, but I'm also concerned about the reputation of my hotel and spa. If the murderer isn't found, and I mean soon, this weekend may be the last time I ever have any guests here at Serenity Hotel and Spa."

Liz stood up, walked over to Judy, and said, "Judy, we'll find the murderer and your hotel and spa will be successful. We just need to get through the next few days. Don't get discouraged." She turned to Roger and said, "Why don't you sit in on the rest of the statements by yourself? I think I'll go up to our room and unpack, plus I need to get Winston situated. He's probably tired of being tied up to the front porch railing, and I'd like to get started on trying to find the person responsible for Nikki's death as soon as possible."

Chief Oliphant stood up, took a business card out of his wallet, and handed it to Liz. "Please call me in the morning. Hopefully, one of us will have found out something that will be relevant to the case.

Thanks for your help."

"I'll talk to you in the morning," Liz said as she walked out the door and over to Judy's assistant who handed her a room key. A short time later she was in their suite down the hall, unpacking and settling in for as long as she was needed.

CHAPTER TEN

Liz had just finished unpacking when Roger walked into the room. "Well, how did the rest of the statements go?" she asked.

"Pretty much as expected. Renee verified Judy's account of the discovery of the body, and the other three women didn't have anything to add. None of them had heard or seen anything. The sirens were the first indication to them that something must be wrong. Naturally, they're in shock. They've been friends for a long, long time."

"Let's sit down for a few minutes, Roger. I'd like to pick your brain. Since you have to leave day after tomorrow, I rather doubt the murderer will be found by then, and I'll be the one doing whatever investigating is needed. Where do you think I should start?"

"First of all, you need to have a heart to heart talk with Judy. Find out what, if anything, Renee told her about all of the women. One of them caused my antenna to go up, because she didn't seem to be as distraught as the others. It may just be her personality, but at the time the chief was taking her statement, I thought it was odd."

"Which one of them was it? I only met them briefly, so they're all kind of blending together in my mind."

"Her name is Amber Ruiz. The chief asked all of them their address and contact information. She lives down in the Central Valley. Her husband's a farmer down there. I was curious about that, because she didn't seem to quite fit in. The others seem to be women of means, although I don't know what Nikki's financial situation was, but Amber seemed to lack their sophistication. There are certainly some big farms down in the Central Valley, but I didn't have the feeling that she and her husband owned one of them. It may be nothing, but I guess I wonder how she got involved with the group."

"Since Renee was bringing her group here for a reunion, maybe she gave Judy a rundown about all of them that would explain how Amber got involved with them. I'll check it out. What else do you think I should do? You're the one with all the years of experience in dealing with crime."

"Yeah, but each case is different. I'd try to find out what I could about Nikki's marital relationship or what was going on in her life that made her so stressed she wanted to visit the sauna before she even unpacked. Maybe she and her husband are having problems. It's that old thing about who has the most to gain when someone is murdered. Oftentimes it's the spouse. Maybe she's very wealthy, and her husband wanted her dead, so he could get his hands on her money. Just throwing things out."

"Roger, what if this isn't about Nikki? What if she was kind of collateral damage?"

He was quiet for several moments while he stroked his chin, seemingly deep in thought. "I think you may be on to something, Liz. Are you thinking maybe this is about Judy and the hotel and spa or even Renee?"

"I'm not really thinking anything. It just crossed my mind. I wonder if either Judy or Renee has any enemies? Maybe someone wanted Judy's hotel and spa to fail for whatever reason, or maybe Renee has a skeleton in her closet. What do you think?"

"I think it definitely should be explored. I'd find out who Judy's competition is and if anyone was worried that if the Serenity Hotel and Spa was successful, it might affect their business. Maybe Renee's ex-husband wanted to get back at her for something that happened in the past. It's a longshot, but worth pursuing."

"Roger, I just thought of something else. Judy and I were talking on the phone one day, and she had to end the call because she had an incoming call. When she called me back, she wasn't very happy. She told me about how a neighbor had been harassing her to let him buy her property. She said something about her assistant letting him inspect the hotel property, and that he wanted to meet with her. Judy told me she'd declined his offers to buy her property several times before, and figured he was going to make another one. I should probably follow up with her on that as well."

"Absolutely. In a case like this when there's nothing solid to go on, you don't want to overlook anything. By the way, we're not going out to dinner tonight. Judy was sure no one would feel like having dinner in a restaurant, and she said she had all the ingredients for clam chowder, and she'd call us when dinner was ready."

"Sounds good. I don't feel like going out for dinner either. I'm very happy to stay here, plus it will be easier for me to talk to Judy. I'm sure the others will probably want to make an early night of it, so I could offer to help her clean up after dinner. Maybe I can find something out then. Roger, do you know if the chief took Nikki's clothes and purse with him?"

"I'm sure he would have. That's pretty standard operating procedure. He'll be looking for names or business cards or anything that might shed some light on this case. Why?"

"For the same reason he took them. There very well might be something in Nikki's purse that could help solve the case. Since we don't know a thing about her and by her own admission, she was stressed, maybe she was involved romantically with another man or something like that."

"That's always a possibility. She probably had a cell phone in her purse, and I'm sure the police will see if there's anything on it that might be relevant."

Just then the phone in the room rang, and Liz walked over and answered it. "We'll be there in a minute, Judy," she said. She turned to Roger and said, "Judy prepared some appetizers and she's opened a bottle of wine. She thought it might take the edge off of everyone's nerves. She'd like all of to meet in the living room."

"Sounds good to me. Let's go. I'm hungrier than I thought, and a glass of wine before dinner sounds wonderful. Ready?"

"As soon as I put on some lipstick. I know this is going to sound weird to you since this is my best friend's hotel, but I'm going to lock the door when we leave. Murders make me nervous."

"You're singing to the choir, Liz. I couldn't agree more."

CHAPTER ELEVEN

Liz, Roger, and Winston walked into the living room and greeted Judy, Renee, and Renee's friends.

"Winston, come here," Judy said, "With everything that's happened today, I haven't had a chance to say hello to you." Winston walked over to where Judy was seated and put his paw on her lap. She patted him on the head and turned to the others in the room. "This dog is the most incredible dog I've ever known. I first met him when I was visiting Liz a day or so after Roger had given him to her. Unfortunately, a murder had taken place in one of the cottages at the Red Cedar Lodge and Spa which Liz owns, and Roger was concerned for Liz's safety, so he gave her Winston to provide protection for Liz when she's alone at the lodge.

"I swear this dog understands everything that anyone says. He's simply amazing. When Roger asked if I'd mind if he and Liz could bring Winston with them when they came this weekend, I didn't even have to think about it. It was an automatic yes."

Roger poured all of them a glass of wine and said, "Maybe we shouldn't have done that, Judy. If word gets out that this is a pet friendly hotel, you might be asking for trouble. Not all pets are going to be as well trained as Winston is."

"I never thought about that, but it probably doesn't make any difference now, since this may be the only time the hotel is ever occupied," Judy said with a glum look of her face.

"Judy, don't get discouraged. We're going to find out who did this, but for now let's enjoy the wine, the dinner, and each other. By the way, this wine is wonderful. I'm not familiar with the vineyard," Roger said.

"Well, if you look out the window over there and down the road a bit, you'll see it. I think I told you once that a neighbor of mine wants to buy my property, so he can expand his vineyard. In fact, he's made me a number of offers to buy it, but I've turned all of them down, because I really want to make a go of this hotel and spa. Anyway, although I can't stand the man, his wine is considered to be the best in the valley, and he and his wife sell out every year just a few months after they bottle it. He brought me two bottles recently when he was making yet another offer. I consider it to be bribe wine, but I have to grudgingly admit it's excellent."

"I can see why he sells out so quickly," Roger said. "This may be the best wine I've ever had. Why don't you like him?"

"The woman I bought the property from told me he'd been trying to buy the property from her for years, and there had been a number of incidents over the years, problems she said, that she attributed to him. She refused to sell it to him and told me she was selling it to me for a lot less than he'd offered her."

"Did she say what the incidents were?" Liz asked.

"Not specifically. She said something about people who worked for her had received threats, and she suspected him of having something to do with a pet cat of hers that mysteriously disappeared. Evidently the cat went outside one day and never came back. She mentioned he told her once that she better sell to him, or she'd regret it. Things of that nature."

"Sounds like someone who might want to see you go out of business. Does he have a wine tasting room?" Roger asked.

"Yes, and since I haven't heard that he's closed it yet due to a lack of inventory, he must still be pouring some wine, but as expensive as his wine is and the way he sells out of it every year, I don't understand why he even bothers with a tasting room. Maybe it's just an ego thing with him."

"I think Liz and I will go there tomorrow under the pretense of tasting some wine and see if we can find out anything."

"Roger, you don't seriously think he could be the murderer, do you? I'm sure he didn't even know Nikki," Judy said.

"That may be true, but even though Nikki was murdered, it might not be about her. It might be about someone not wanting you to make your hotel and spa a success." He turned to Renee and continued, "Renee, I hate to say this, but since you were the one who scheduled this reunion weekend to be held here at Judy's hotel and spa, maybe it was someone who has it in for you."

"You're kidding, Roger. How could I possibly be involved in something like Nikki's murder?" she asked.

"I have no idea, but I'd like you to think about it, and see if you can come up with any names of people who are jealous of you or could possibly be considered enemies. Not saying you have any, just saying if there is anyone you can think of, let's put it on the table."

"Speaking of tables," Judy said, "it's time to eat. By the way, Roger, in case you were wondering, Renee has told me that in spite of Nikki's tragic death, she and her friends have decided to stay here for the weekend as they'd planned. She's already paid for the treatments, and I've hired the spa personnel."

"Yes, we're definitely going to stay, right?" Renee said to her friends who nodded in agreement. "There's nothing we can do, so we might as well spend some time together. I think tonight will be an early night, since Judy told me our first treatments are scheduled for 9:00 in the morning, and she serves breakfast from 7:30 to 9:00."

They stood up, walked into the dining room, and sat down in front of the steaming bowls of clam chowder Judy's assistant had placed on the table. A tossed green salad was next to each bowl along with plates at each end of the table piled high with warm sourdough bread.

They were quiet for a few moments while they tasted the soup. "Judy, this is the best clam chowder I've ever had. Did you make it or did your assistant?"

"Thanks, Roger, and yes, I did make it. It's an old family recipe, and I agree with you that it's really good. I still think it's the best I've ever had even if I did make it. I know they serve clam chowder in all of the restaurants on the wharf in San Francisco, but I think what makes this one so good is that I put about twice as many clams in it than most other recipes call for, and I like to use the whole baby clams. So many of the recipes call for diced or minced clams to be put in it, and while they call it clam chowder, you're lucky if you can even find one in it."

Roger turned to Liz and said, "I think you better get this recipe, if Judy will give it to you. It would be great served at the Red Cedar Lodge." He turned to Judy and said, "Any chance you'd share it with Liz?"

"Of course, I'll run a copy off for Liz after dinner."

"Perfect. In exchange, Liz and I will help you clean up the dishes. The rest of you can go get your beauty sleep, so you'll be rested for your spa treatments in the morning."

CHAPTER TWELVE

"Judy, you look exhausted. Why don't you sit at the kitchen table while Roger and I do the dishes? Winston would be more than happy to sit next to you. Right now, you look like you could use some dog therapy, and he's very good at that."

"Thanks, Liz. I think I'll take you up on that. Winston, come here," Judy said as she sat down at the table and motioned for the big boxer to sit next to her. He seemed to sense that she was very concerned about the events of the day and began licking her hand.

"Judy, you mentioned that your neighbor wanted to buy this property. Your refusal to sell to him could possibly provide a motive for him to discredit you and your business. That would make it more likely you would be willing to sell to him, but have you thought of anyone else who might want to see you fail?"

"Roger, I've been wracking my brain ever since we discovered Nikki, and I can't think of anyone."

"What about one of your ex-husbands?" he asked knowing that Judy had been married three times. He brought in more dishes for Liz to rinse and put in the dishwasher, as he asked Judy questions.

"No, that's a dead end. I never see them or hear from them unless it's at a wedding, a graduation, or a funeral, and then it's very civil.

Actually, I would say that all three have nothing but good things to say about me. Although I'm obviously not married to them now, I was lucky to part with all of them on an amicable basis."

"Judy, ever since I've known you, and from what Liz has told me, there's rarely been a time when a man wasn't in your life. What's been happening lately on that front?"

"Not much. Sure, I've been out with several different men since I moved to Calistoga, but there's been nothing serious with any of them."

"Is there any man presently in your life?" Roger asked pausing at the door before he went out to bring in another load of dishes from the dining room.

"I've been seeing one man for the past few weeks, but I can't think of any reason why he would be involved in something like Nikki's murder."

"Tell us about him," Liz said as she continued to load the dishwasher.

"My daughter was visiting me several weeks ago, and we went to a new French restaurant in Yountville for lunch. There were three men at the table next to us who were sharing a bottle of wine. I realized it was the same wine Brigitte and I had ordered, so I asked them how it was. One thing led to another and we ended up talking to them throughout lunch. Two of the men left and while the third one was paying his bill, he mentioned that he'd recently moved to Calistoga.

"I told him I was a new resident as well. We shared what each of us did and then he said, 'I'm having the home I bought completely renovated. My mother is going to live with me when I'm finished with it, but it still needs some more work before that happens.' Anyway, he said that his wife had passed away several years ago, and he'd love to have a woman's opinion on the room he was having decorated for his mother and asked Brigitte and me if we had time to follow him to his home and give him our opinion."

"You met some guy in a restaurant, and you followed him home?" Roger asked incredulously.

"Roger, you can drop those raised eyebrows. I said I had my daughter with me, plus we were in my car, and I decided if I didn't like the looks of the area he was driving to, I could always stop following him. I honestly didn't think the guy could even afford to eat in that restaurant. He was wearing a t-shirt, and I was a little nervous about where he lived. Believe me, it was completely innocent."

Roger turned to Liz. "Did you do things like follow strange men to their homes before I met you?" he asked.

"Roger, I'm not Judy. She's never met a man who didn't like her. No, I did not follow strange men to their homes, but in full disclosure, I never had one ask me to."

"Roger, this conversation is going nowhere. I'll just close it by saying that Sam, that's his name, didn't live in a house, he lived in a mansion on twenty-three acres of prime Napa Valley real estate. His mother's room was not a room, it was a huge suite. It was absolutely incredible, and he couldn't have been nicer. He even gave me a case of olive oil that was produced on his property. I've been seeing him a couple of times a week since then. There is absolutely no way he could have been involved in this. He doesn't want this property, and our relationship hasn't gotten to the point where I could make him love me or hate me. Trust me, that's a dead-end."

"Judy," Liz said laughing, "the one thing you've never done in all the years I've known you is bore me. Only you could go to a restaurant and end up seeing a man who must be one of the wealthiest men in Napa Valley and from what I hear, that's saying a lot."

"Okay, Judy, we'll let Sam rest," Roger said. "Since you don't seem to have anyone you can think of who would want to see you fail other than your neighbor, what about Renee? Does she have any enemies? What about her ex-husband?"

"I've known Renee for about as long as I've known Liz and in all that time, I don't think I've ever heard a bad word about her. She's involved in more charities than I have fingers and toes, and she gives generously to each of them. She is one of the nicest people I've ever met. Her children and grandchildren adore her," she said as a cloud seemed to pass over her face.

Liz knew that two of Judy's children had struggled with drug abuse problems as well as being college dropouts. She and Judy had talked about it many times over the years, and Liz had suggested several times that Judy quit bailing them out of whatever mess they were in and let them fend for themselves. As far as she knew, Judy was still bailing them out. Her daughter, a psychologist, was the light of Judy's life, and Liz was glad that at least she had a good relationship with her.

"What about Renee's ex-husband?" Roger asked.

"I don't think she's seen him in years other than at some San Francisco charity gala or something like that. She's been divorced a number of years, and from what she's told me, he's very happy with the woman he subsequently married, and they have two children. She told me once that the one redeeming feature her ex-husband has is that he's remained a good father to his and Renee's children over the years, and for that she was grateful."

"From what you've told me so far, we have a big zero on the suspect list for Renee and pretty much for you other than your neighbor. Let's look at the other women and Nikki herself. Do you know anything about them?"

"Only what Renee told me on the phone when she originally made the reservations. Since Liz just put the last of the dishes in the dishwasher, let's go in the living room, and I'll tell you what she told me." She stood up and they followed her into the living room, Winston bringing up the rear.

CHAPTER THIRTEEN

"The kitchen chairs are fine, but these are far more comfortable," Judy said sitting down in a soft wingback chair. Although the Serenity Hotel was a large two-story yellow and white Victorian style structure, which had been added onto several times over the years, Judy had the furniture custom-made to ensure it would be comfortable but still fit in with the Victorian style of architecture. It had been an expensive undertaking, but she wanted her guests to enjoy themselves, and she and her decorator had made sure that the furnishings in all of the rooms in the hotel accomplished that goal.

Roger and Liz each sat in a large chair near Judy's with Winston at their feet between them. "Okay, Judy, I'd like you to tell us everything Renee told you about her friends."

Judy relayed the conversation she'd had a few weeks earlier with Renee and concluded by saying, "That's all I know. They arrived maybe an hour or so before you got here. I was busy telling them about the spa and getting them registered and in their rooms, so I never really had a chance to talk to them individually."

"Tiffany and Nancy seem to fit in with Renee, as far as money, social status, and sophistication are concerned. I'm having trouble understanding how Amber fits in with the others, and from what you told us about her, I'm wondering why she continues to come to the reunions," Roger said.

"I think I can answer that," Liz said. "Roger, think about it, whether you're a man or a woman, you hate to admit your friends fared better in life than you did. It sounds like she didn't make much of her life, but she doesn't want to admit it, so she continues to attend the reunions."

"I can understand that, Liz, but what I don't understand is why she didn't express a lot more remorse about Nikki's death. I wonder if there was bad blood between them. Are you sure Renee didn't say something to you about their relationship?"

"No, not a thing," Judy replied "but I agree, she doesn't seem to fit in with the others. Something I wondered about is when Nikki got here, she sure didn't look like she was from money either. She was wearing a faded skirt and cheap blouse that looked like she'd probably gotten both of them on sale at a discount store, and not one of the better ones, at that."

"Renee told you there was some sort of scandal involving her husband and his real estate development business. Since you lived in San Francisco and traveled with Renee's crowd, did you ever hear anything about that?" Roger asked.

"No. Her husband was in real estate development, and I only have one friend whose husband is involved in it. I suppose I could find out Nikki's husband's name and ask my friend if she knows anything."

"I think that would be a good idea. From what Renee told you it seems that when Nikki was living in San Francisco she was quite wealthy and involved in a lot of the same charities that Renee was. Her husband must have likewise been pretty well off. Did she mention anything about him?"

"She told me they'd attended a number of charity galas and things like that over the years, but their circles of friends were different, so she never had a chance to get to know him."

"Did she say anything about the talk that must have gone on after they left town and there were rumors of a scandal involving her husband?" Liz asked.

"I know it seems pretty unbelievable given Renee's social status and money, but I've never known her to gossip. If she's your friend, that's it. She doesn't get involved in gossip, simple as that. Since Nikki was part of her group, I would imagine if someone had said something about her or her husband, Renee would have stopped the person from continuing."

"It sure might have helped solve this murder if she'd listened instead," Roger grumbled. He looked at his watch. "It's getting late, and we all need to get some sleep. I want to find out as much as I can in the next day and a half before I have to leave. Judy, would you ask Renee what Nikki's husband's name is and then call your friend? At least we can start with that. Liz, I'd like you to come with me tomorrow afternoon when I go to the tasting room next door, and don't forget you need to talk to the chief tomorrow morning. Maybe he's found out something. Winston, come, you need to go outside before we head off to bed. Judy, see you in the morning."

"I told you I have a great breakfast cook, so be sure and eat here. She's really something," Judy said standing up and turning the lamps off in the room. "Good night, and I'm so glad you two are here. I really don't think I could have faced this by myself, although I am surprised we haven't been inundated with the press."

"Chief Oliphant said he wasn't going to release any information regarding Nikki's death until her husband was notified. The press may be here tomorrow. Good night, Judy," Liz said.

"Good night. Oh, darn it, I forgot to run off that recipe. I'll get it for you in the morning."

CHAPTER FOURTEEN

The next morning Roger looked out the window and said, "Liz, it looks like another beautiful day. I'll feed Winston and then take him outside while you're getting dressed. Meet you in the dining room. Come on, Winston, time for an outside and breakfast."

A few minutes later Liz walked into the dining room where Roger was waiting at a table for her, drinking coffee. She looked at a nearby serving table that had been set up with a buffet breakfast on it. "Roger, I'm not even going to bother to sit down. This food looks wonderful. Judy wasn't kidding when she said she'd hired a great breakfast cook."

Roger joined her at the buffet table and began filling his plate. "I don't know what else is in these little ham and egg things, but if they taste half as good as they look, I'll be a very happy man," Roger said.

"I agree. I'll have to see if I can get this recipe from Judy as well," she said as she helped herself to a large spoonful of fresh fruit and a muffin. The cook had written down the names of the various dishes and put them in place card holders in front of each item. According to the card, the muffin Liz had chosen was made with bananas and walnuts. Liz served a lot of muffins at her lodge and was always on the lookout for a new recipe. She was pretty sure this was another one she'd be asking for.

"Liz, when you're asking Judy for recipes, see if she'll give you the one for the frozen cantaloupe mousse we had for dessert last night. That left a great taste in my mouth. I really liked it."

They'd just put their plates down on the table when a young woman walked over and said to Liz, "Good morning, I'm Nettie. May I get you some coffee or juice, ma'am?"

"I'll take some coffee, and I imagine my husband would like some orange juice. Would I be right, Roger?"

"Definitely, thank you."

"Are you sure you don't want some, ma'am? It's fresh squeezed."

"Well, in that case, how can I turn it down? Yes, I would like some, thanks."

A few moments later Nettie returned with their juice and Liz's coffee. "Let me know when you'd like another cup. You can ring this little bell, and I'll come right out of the kitchen. Enjoy your breakfast. You're the last guests to arrive for breakfast this morning. The others wanted to eat early, so they could get to their treatments on time." She walked away and disappeared into the kitchen, closing the kitchen door behind her.

"Liz, after breakfast, I'm going to drive into town and get a lay of the land. I've never been to Calistoga before. I know it's a small town, but that's about it. I won't be gone long."

"That's fine. Why don't you take Winston with you? He loves to ride in the car, and I need to talk to Chief Oliphant. Hopefully, I'll have some information when you return."

"Okay, but you have one thing to do that's even more important than talking to the chief and that's to get Judy's recipes. I didn't know she was such a good cook."

"Hate to spoil the illusion, Roger, but I'd be willing to bet that most of the recipes are her cook's. Other than clam chowder, I'm not sure Judy knows how to cook. When I lived in San Francisco and we became friends, she was famous for eating whatever she'd brought home the night before from when she'd been treated to dinner by her most recent male flavor of the month. I'm not sure the oven in her house has ever been turned on, and her inability to cook almost anything was an ongoing joke among her friends. I'm still surprised she opened a hotel and spa. She's about the most undomestic person I've ever known, but I have to say she's done it up right here at Serenity Hotel. If we can get this murder solved, I predict she's going to be very successful."

"She has the one trait that a good hotelier needs, and that is she sincerely loves to talk to people and be with them. She's so friendly and warm people can't help but be drawn to her."

"We have to solve this murder if for no other reason than I really want her to make a success of the hotel and spa. I've known her for many years, and as I told you, she's never worked. This is a first for her, and I'm really proud of her for tackling it. It's not about the money she'll make, it's about doing something that will make her feel successful."

"I agree, and although I won't be here much longer, I think you need to stay for however long it takes to solve it. I think I'll rent a car tomorrow and leave mine here for you."

"Roger, I'd be willing to bet Judy has an extra one in the garage. She loves cars, and that was something else we always kidded her about. We were always asking her why one woman needed two or three cars. Her answer was that she never knew which one she'd feel like driving until she went out to her garage."

"In that case, I'll see if she'll loan me one for a few days. Winston and I are off, see you later," he said as he bent down and kissed her. "See what you can do to find the bad guy, but don't get into trouble doing it."

"Roger, you know me better than that. I'd never get into trouble solving a murder."

"My lovely Liz, you forget that I have a very good memory, and when it comes to you and murder, I well remember how lucky you've been. I think you have some kind of a special angel that's assigned to do nothing but look out for you. Anyway, that's the only thing I can think of to explain how you've come through unscathed in so many situations involving a murder."

"You and Winston have fun in town."

CHAPTER FIFTEEN

After she finished her breakfast, Liz knocked on the kitchen door and heard someone say, "Come in." She opened the door and walked in. A woman wearing an apron was standing by the sink, and Nettie was standing next to her.

"Hi, I'm Liz Langley. You must be the cook. I just wanted to tell you how much my husband and I enjoyed breakfast. It was excellent. I own a lodge and a spa on the coast north of San Francisco, and I know how difficult it is to cook for a number of people. Thank you. This was a wonderful way to start the day out."

The cook walked over to Liz and said, "My name's Mary. I'm not really a chef, but I do like to cook and eat. I'm so glad you enjoyed it, particularly because this is the first morning I've cooked for guests. During the last month, I've been cooking for Mrs. Rasmussen, and we've been taste testing and deciding what we wanted to put out for breakfast for the guests. I wanted to find out what she liked best, so I could serve it to her guests when she opened for business, although I understand from Mrs. Rasmussen that there was an incident yesterday that could affect the future of the hotel and spa."

"If you call murder an incident, yes, it could affect the spa, but I'm confident that the murderer will be found within a few days and then Judy can concentrate on filling the hotel and spa with guests. With your cooking, the way Judy has renovated and furnished the hotel, and what I assume will be wonderful experiences at the spa, I'm sure this will soon become the place to go in the Napa Valley for people who want to rest and recharge."

"I hope you're right. I saw an article about the murder in the paper, and when I got here early this morning, there were several reporters. I told them 'no comment' when they asked what I knew, and I told them to leave, that they were on private property, and not welcome here. I knew Mrs. Rasmussen wouldn't want that kind of publicity on her opening weekend."

"Absolutely not. It was nice meeting you, and if you would allow me to have a couple of recipes, particularly the ones for the banana walnut muffins and those little mini egg and ham casseroles, I'd really appreciate it."

"I'm glad you liked them. Let me check with Mrs. Rasmussen, but I'm sure she'll say I can give them to you."

"I would imagine she will. See you tomorrow," Liz said as she walked out the door and went down the hall to the suite where she and Roger were staying. The large honeymoon suite was the only accommodation for guests on the first floor and looked out on a private garden with vined walls and colorful flowers spilling out of containers. A king-sized canopied bed was in the bedroom and armchairs, a television, and a desk were in an adjacent room. A large white clawfoot bathtub was in the middle of the bathroom with a modern shower occupying the corner. Next to the bathtub was a bench piled high with fluffy white towels and spa products. Pillar candles were in all the rooms.

What a way to start a marriage or even re-energize one, Liz thought as she unlocked the door and looked out at the flowers and vines in the private garden. *It's absolutely delightful, and I feel like I'm miles from anywhere.*

She walked into the room where the desk was and sat down in front of it. She took the police chief's card out of her purse and called the number he had given her. It was his direct line.

"Chief Oliphant here," the masculine voice said.

"Chief, it's Liz Langley. I know you're leaving in a couple of hours, and I wanted to fill you in on what I've learned so far." She relayed the conversation she'd had with Judy the evening before. "I figured that you'd located her husband and told him, since the press was here very early this morning, and it was in the Calistoga News."

He listened and then said, "Yes, her husband was informed of her death last night. We found a business card in Mrs. Evans' purse with the name of Damon Evans on it. We were pretty sure it was her husband, because the company was located in Sacramento, where she lived. I called the Sacramento police chief, and even though it was late, he sent one of his men to their apartment to inform Mr. Evans of his wife's death. The policeman told me that although Mr. Evans said he was heartbroken, the officer didn't feel it was at all sincere and thought it was more like some sort of contrived act. He said it might be a good idea to follow up and see where he was at the time of the murder. I'll do that when I get back from my vacation. I don't have time now."

"My husband and I can do it for you. We'll go over there this afternoon and see what we can find out. What kind of business was he in?"

"The business card said AAA Heating and Air Conditioning on it. Under Damon Evans' name were the words 'Installer' so I guess he installs heating and air conditioning equipment for the business. I had one of my men look it up on the Internet, and the business has been around for many years. Kind of interesting he'd be working there now and from what you told me, it seems there was some kind of scandal about him when he was living in San Francisco. I wonder what that was all about."

"I should have some information about that later today. Mrs. Rasmussen is going to call a friend of hers whose husband is in real estate development and see what she can find out."

"Good idea. I'd like to know more about that. Spouses always bear looking into when murder's involved."

"That's about all the news I have, Chief. I would like her husband's address, and do you want to call me tonight or do you want me to call you?"

"I better call you. Finding enough bars on my cell phone to get a signal can be tricky in the area where I'm going, and I may have to leave the campsite to do that. What would be a good time for me to call? Here's her husband's address."

Liz wrote it down and said, "Whatever works for you. I'll keep my phone with me, although if you could call around eight or so, I might have more information for you. We were planning on going to the wine tasting room next door this afternoon, but I think we better go to Sacramento first and do that when we return. I don't know what time they close."

"That's fine. I'll call you around then, but I do want to caution you about something. A murder has been committed, and that means a murderer is on the loose. I want you to be very careful when you talk to people. The last thing I want is for something to happen to you. Am I making myself clear?"

"Yes, Chief, and I have to tell you that you sound exactly like my husband. Let me put you at ease. Shortly after I first met Roger I became involved in solving a murder mystery. Like you, Roger was concerned for my safety, and he purchased a large boxer guard dog for me. The dog pretty much goes everywhere with me, particularly if I'm involved in something like this, so Winston will be going to Sacramento with us, and if we can get him in, he'll even sit next to me in the wine tasting room."

"You didn't hear this from me, Liz, but there's a little shop in town, The Dog Spa, that carries therapy dog items. You might want to get one of those blanket-type things and put it around your dog. You know, one that says Therapy Dog in Training. That should get him into the tasting room."

"Thanks, Chief, and if anyone ever asks, I'll deny we ever had this conversation."

"What conversation, Liz?" the chief asked just before the line went dead.

CHAPTER SIXTEEN

Liz decided to spend some time making notes of what she needed to do. She had just written, "Call Roger's private investigator at the firm" when she heard a knock on her door. She walked over to it and asked, "Who is it?"

"Liz, it's Judy. Open the door. I talked to my friend in San Francisco and found out some interesting stuff." Liz opened the door and a breathless Judy hurried in. "You know, Liz, part of me is sick about this, but the other part of me is kind of excited. Remember when we traveled to Washington and were responsible for the police catching the woman who'd murdered the mayor's wife in cottage number six at your spa? Well, this is kind of like that. It's scary to think it happened here, but on the other hand it's kind of exciting to be involved in something like you see on TV. Know what I mean?"

"Afraid I don't share your enthusiasm for murder, Judy, but yes, I do know what you mean. Sit down and tell me what you found out. Oh, before you start, your cook is going to ask you for permission to give me a couple of her recipes. I hope you'll say yes."

"Of course, now, here's what I found out from my friend. Evidently it was quite the scandal. I find it hard to believe that Renee didn't know about it, but you know, like I told you she's…"

"Judy, you're rambling. I want to know exactly what your friend said."

"Okay. Damon Evans was really big in the real estate development world. He worked for one of the largest companies in the Bay Area. She said his wife, Nikki, and he lived a very good life there. Their pictures were in the paper all the time, and he made a lot of money. My friend has a lot of money so when she says that Damon made a lot of money, it had to have been a whole lot of money."

"Judy, from what you told me, you didn't seem to think Nikki looked like she had money, and you also told me Renee didn't think she did. What happened?"

"Evidently Damon was caught with his hand in the cookie jar, or should I say two cookie jars. He was taking bribe money from different contractors and bidders for upcoming projects as well as holding money back that was supposed to go into the company's funds. In other words, he was embezzling money from his employer."

"Did she give you any idea how much was involved?"

"Evidently it was in the millions. According to my friend, the head of the company where he worked told Damon he was going to the police with the evidence and that Damon would go to prison for a long time. He said the only way Damon could save himself from going to prison was to pay the money back."

"Wow. Since he's not in prison, he must have paid it back. Where did he get that much?"

"According to my friend, he sold the house he and Nikki owned. Even though they owed a lot on it, it was in Hillsborough, one of the most exclusive suburbs of San Francisco, and according to her, even though they got a bundle for it, it still wasn't enough."

"So where did he get the rest of the money from?"

"My friend said this is pretty much speculation, but she's certain that Nikki must have given it to him, because her parents died around that time, and she was an only child. My friend said Nikki's parents were apparently quite wealthy." Judy sat back with a satisfied smile on her face and looked like a child that needed to be told they'd done a good job.

"Nice work, Judy. Did your friend say anything about where Damon worked now?"

"Yes, she said he really got his comeuppance. No one in the real estate development industry would hire him, so he was forced to do what he did when he was in college, work as an installer in heating and air conditioning. Can you imagine? Here he and Nikki were really bucks up, and then they had to leave San Francisco under a dark cloud of suspicion and go to Sacramento where he was forced to work as an installer for some heating and air conditioning company to make money to live on. I wonder why Nikki stayed with him."

"Good question. If I meet him I'm going to ask him."

"What are you talking about?" Judy asked.

Liz told Judy about her conversation with the chief and that she wanted to go to Sacramento and then return to Calistoga and visit the wine tasting room.

"You know I'm not the best cook around, but my father was a bird hunter, and one of the few things I know how to make, other than clam chowder, is a great pheasant dish. Since you're probably going to be tired with everything you have planned this afternoon, why don't you and Roger join me for dinner? Sam, you know, the guy I've been seeing, is a hunter, and he gave me some pheasants recently. Renee and her group are going into town for dinner tonight, so it will be just the three of us. Okay with you?"

"Sounds wonderful. I haven't had pheasant in a long time. Plan on it." Liz heard the sound of a dog walking on the hardwood floor in the hall and said, "I think Winston has returned and if he's here,

Roger must be too. I need to tell him what I've found out, and then we need to drive over to Sacramento."

She opened the door and Winston ran into the room, sniffed to make sure she was safe, sat down next to her, and waited for Roger to catch up.

"See you tonight," Judy said as she turned towards the door. "Be careful."

"I heard that," Roger said. "It always makes me nervous when someone says be careful to Liz. Elizabeth, what have you done now?"

"See you both at dinner," Judy said as she walked out into the hall.

"I'll fill you in on what our plans are for the rest of the day, and there's nothing to be nervous about. Promise."

"When you say that, it makes me doubly nervous," Roger said.

CHAPTER SEVENTEEN

"Roger, I had a long talk with Chief Oliphant, and we agreed that you and I need to go to Sacramento and see if we can talk to Damon Evans."

"So the chief was able to find him and tell him about Nikki?" Roger asked as he changed into a short-sleeved shirt. Even though it wasn't even noon, the weather had turned uncommonly warm.

"Yes, and here's something interesting. It turns out that Nikki's husband is a heating and air conditioning installer. It kind of makes him a suspect to my way of thinking. I'm sure he'd know how to control the heat in a sauna and even how to make it hot enough for someone to die."

"Liz, I'm not following you. Is this the husband Nikki was married to when she lived in San Francisco? The guy Judy said was in some kind of a scandal? That's a big leap from being a high roller in real estate development to someone who installs heating units and air conditioners. I've obviously missed something."

"No, it's the same man. Here's what Judy found out and what the chief told me about her husband." She recounted both of the conversations to Roger.

"All right, I suppose there could be a tie-in here, but right now you have a lot of suppositions, rather than facts. You still have a lot to discover to ever have him tied to the murder."

"I agree, Roger, but here's my plan. I thought we'd drive over to Sacramento and see if we can talk to him. I'll come up with some reason why we're doing it. I'd really like to know where he was about the time she was murdered. Since it was a weekday afternoon, maybe he was working and he has a legitimate alibi. In that case, we won't waste any more time on him. After we finish with him, I thought we'd come back to Calistoga, go to the winery down the road, and see what we can find out there, but first we have to go a place called The Dog Spa which is located here in town. I can be ready in a few minutes. Sound okay to you?"

"Whoa, I'm fine with going to Sacramento and trying to track down Nikki's husband, and I'm fine with going wine tasting at the vineyard next door, but I'm missing something about a need to go to The Dog Spa. We brought plenty of food for Winston, and I'm even sure there's enough for the extra time you'll be spending here after I leave."

"Roger, we'll pretend we're not having the conversation we're about to have because I told Chief Oliphant that I never had that conversation with him."

Roger held his hand up in front of him. "I thought I was lost a few minutes ago, but now I'm totally lost. What in the devil are you talking about?"

She told him about the non-conversation she'd had with the chief regarding her safety, Winston, and the chief's recommendation.

"Liz, I really don't think the people who work with therapy dogs would appreciate you putting something on Winston that says he's a therapy dog, when he's never been trained to be one. That's not fair to those hard-working trainers, and I'm not comfortable with it. I'm going to have to veto that idea."

Liz was quiet for a few moments and then she said, "Okay, I understand what you're saying, but as smart as Winston is, I bet he could be a therapy dog."

"Thinking he could be and actually being one are quite different, like a year's worth of work or something different," Roger said, petting Winston who seemed to sense they were talking about him.

"Let's do a compromise. I promise I won't buy him something that says he actually is a therapy dog, or a therapy dog in training. That's the compromise I'll make with you. In return, I'd still like to go to The Dog Spa and see if I can find something else that would work. Don't you think that's a fair compromise?"

"When you put it that way it does seem to be, but I'll reserve judgment until we leave The Dog Spa."

"Sounds good to me. I'm ready to go. Let me pull up the address on my smart phone. Since you've already been to town, you probably have some sense of where streets are. It's a pretty small town."

A few minutes later Roger parked on the street in front of The Dog Spa. The sign in the front window said "Dogs Welcome." Roger attached a leash to Winston's collar, and the three of them entered the store. It was Saturday and from the number of people in the store, the owners of dogs in Calistoga were certainly adding to the city's economy.

They looked around the store for a few minutes while Winston and a few other dogs took turns sniffing each other to decide whether or not they were suitable for being in the store. They all passed some unwritten test that is known to dogs but not to humans.

Liz walked over to a woman who was standing behind the counter next to the cash register. "Excuse me," she said, "but I need for my dog to occasionally go into establishments where dogs are usually not allowed. He's not a therapy dog, but I was wondering if you have anything that might help me get him in."

Roger shook his head in disbelief when he heard what Liz was saying. The woman came out from behind the counter and said, "I do have something that might work for a situation like that. We sell them as cute little stocking stuffers or things for the dog owner who has everything. It's a certificate that says "… has been certified by me, Dr. William Smith, to be a comfort dog for his owner and by state law is permitted to be with his owner to prevent anxiety." She turned to Liz and said, "I think this would be perfect for you."

"I'll take it," Liz said. "Thank you so much. You just solved a big problem for me." She paid the woman and the three of them left the store.

When they were in the car Roger turned to her and said, "Liz, do you really think something like that would work? You know that you don't suffer from anxiety."

"That's true, Roger, but other people don't know that. The last time I was on a plane there was a woman in front of me who had a small dog at her feet. I overheard the stewardesses talking when I went back to the restroom. One of them was angry that the woman had brought the dog on the plane and said the passenger sure didn't look like she was suffering from anxiety. The other stewardess said that was the new rule. It really didn't matter what they thought, and although she knew the new rule was being abused by most of the people who brought their dogs on planes, occasionally it probably did help a passenger be less anxious during the flight.

"Liz, I think that's about the most far-fetched thing I've ever heard of, but technically you kept your end of the bargain. Write Winston's name on the certificate, so you don't get caught when you're entering the winery."

"Or anywhere else I might choose to take him."

"Elizabeth…"

CHAPTER EIGHTEEN

Liz and Roger easily found the apartment building in Sacramento where Damon Evans lived. It looked like it had seen better days. The lawn, if one could call it that, was filled with weeds, and the sidewalk leading up to the front door was cracked. There were several sacks of trash stacked up on the front porch. They tried the front door to the building, but it was locked.

Just then a man walked up to the door and said, "Excuse me. I live here, and you have to have a key to get in. Are you looking for someone in particular?"

"Yes, we want to talk to Damon Evans. Do you know which apartment is his?"

"I do," the man said, "but he's not here. I live in the apartment next to him. He left for Nic's a couple of hours ago. Probably won't be home 'til late tonight. Want me to tell him you were here?"

"No, what and where is Nic's?" Roger asked. "We'll see if we can find him there."

"It's a neighborhood bar two streets over. Damon practically supports it. Matter of fact, I think Nic would have to close it down if it wasn't for Damon. He's there almost every week night and most of Saturday and Sunday, too. You can't miss it. Do you know him?"

"No, we've not met him. Is there anything you can tell me about him?" Liz asked.

"Well, you won't be able to miss him with the beard he's grown. He's lived here about two years now, and I've been watching that grey beard just get longer and longer, although I will say he keeps it well trimmed. When I saw him earlier today he told me his wife had died, so I'm sure he's drowning his sorrows at the moment, although from the way they argued, I can't imagine he's all that sorry."

"I never knew his wife. What was she like?" Liz asked.

"Classy lady. Seemed too good for him, and I always had the sense she let him know it. She didn't seem like she belonged in this neighborhood, but then again neither did he. Goes to show, you just never know about people."

"What did they argue about?" Liz asked.

"Pretty much everything. I couldn't help but overhear them because the air conditioning in the apartment house is spotty. I knew Damon worked for a company that specialized in air conditioning and heating, and I asked him once why he didn't do something about it. He told me the owner said he wouldn't pay Damon to fix it, and Damon didn't want to do it for free. Can't say that I blame him.

"Anyway, back to the arguing. I guess he was some big deal when they lived in San Francisco. One time I heard her say something about the money she'd given him, so he wouldn't have to go to jail. Another time I heard her tell him she should have left him a long time ago. He told her the only reason she'd stayed with him was because he'd been stupid enough to marry her when she was knocked up. He said he was pretty sure it wasn't his kid, but he'd been too young and dumb to find out if it really was his. He said it was a good thing she'd lost it, because if it hadn't looked like him, he would have thrown her and the kid out."

"Wow," Liz said. "That does not sound like a happy marriage."

"Tell me about it. The only way we can often get some relief from this heat in the summertime is to open our doors to the hallway. You can't help but hear things that would probably be better left unheard."

"Yes, it sounds like you heard a lot more than they were aware of," Roger said.

"I did. I guess he had some legal problems in San Francisco, and she inherited some money and bailed him out, but I never did know exactly what it was about."

"Now that his wife is dead, I wonder if he'll stay here," Liz said.

"I don't know. This apartment ain't much, but the rent's cheap, and I don't think Damon can afford to move up, plus he's got all his so-called friends at Nic's. At least he has a place to go while he lives here."

"Well, he could always drive there, if he didn't move too far away," Liz said.

The man laughed and said, "I wouldn't want to be on the road with Damon driving after he's spent the evening drinking at Nic's, believe me. I could tell you things..." The alarm on his watch went off, and he looked down at it. "I'd like to talk to you, but I've got some ice cream in this sack, and if I stay here any longer, it's going to melt, plus I've got a meeting I need to get to. Good luck with Damon," he said as he walked into the building.

"If we're going into some sleazy bar to try to talk to a possible murderer, I may actually be glad you bought that certificate. I do have the gun I'm authorized to carry with me, but I'll feel a lot better knowing that Winston is with us as well," Roger said. "And please don't say I told you so or something cute like that."

"My lips are sealed."

"Uhh-huh," Roger said rolling his eyes.

CHAPTER NINETEEN

They drove two blocks, and Roger turned down the street where Nic's was located. It was impossible to miss the neighborhood bar. The building was painted burnt orange and had a blue door with a tattered yellow canopy which had clearly seen better days. The effect was that of someone trying to copy the style of a Tuscany building, but hadn't been able to pull it off. A large ashtray was sitting on a bench next to the door, filled with cigarette butts from drinkers who needed to smoke but had to go outside the bar to do so.

Roger held Winston's leash as they walked into the dark room. A man behind the bar said in a strong voice, "Sorry, no dogs allowed in here."

Roger walked over to the bar and said, "I know it sounds silly, but my wife has a certificate from her doctor indicating she gets anxious and needs to have the dog with her. He provides comfort. Liz, show him the certificate."

Liz opened her purse to get it out, and the man said, "As long as the dog is trained, I guess it's okay. What can I get you?"

"We'll both have whatever's on tap," Roger said, knowing that Liz hated beer and would have preferred a soft drink, but he also knew that this was the type of establishment where one didn't order soft drinks.

Liz looked around at the Saturday afternoon crowd of drinkers who were watching a San Francisco Giants baseball game on a television which hung on the wall behind the bar. No one paid any attention to them. She spotted Damon sitting at the far end of the bar. His grey beard easily gave him away. Roger saw him at the same time and nodded his head towards Damon as he walked over and took a seat next to him. Liz joined him and sat on a stool at the corner of the bar. The bartender brought them two beers in frosted mugs.

Roger raised his glass and said, "Here's to San Francisco and you, my love." He said it loud enough for Damon to hear, but since the television was turned on full blast no one else in the room heard it.

Damon turned to him and said, "You from San Francisco? I used to live there."

"I lived there until two years ago, when I moved to Red Cedar on the coast north of there. Still think it's a beautiful city even if it does get a bad rap from time to time. And you, you ever live there?" Roger asked.

"Yeah, and I sure wish I was back there. Had a pretty good life then, but I ran into some problems and decided it was time for me to leave the city by the bay."

"Looks like you're running on empty there," Roger said. "Let me buy you a beer. Anyone who likes San Francisco is a friend of mine." He motioned the bartender over and said, "One for my friend here. Thanks."

"I appreciate that. I'm having a hard time today. My wife died yesterday. Sure didn't expect that. Think I'm in a bit of shock. Actually, the policeman who told me about it last night said she was murdered. Glad I've got an alibi. She and I'd been married too long, and we argued a bit. If anyone had heard us, they might think I was the one who did it. He said the time of death was about 2:30 in the afternoon. Good thing I was here from noon till about 7:00 when I realized I'd had too much to drink and went home about 7:00.

Around 7:30 or so, the cop showed up and told me. You'll vouch for me, right, Nic?" he said to the bartender as he put a fresh beer mug in front of Damon.

"Pretty much like what you do every afternoon and night," Nic said. "I can vouch you were here, and I certainly appreciate your business. Neighborhood bars like this one are probably on their way out. The young people all want to go where the action is, kind of a see and be seen thing. No one's going to be seen too much in a bar like Nic's."

"I'm sorry to hear about your wife," Roger said to Damon. "Are you going to stay here or go back to San Francisco?"

"It's a long story, but I'm kind of persona non-grata, you know, someone who isn't real welcome there. Had a lot of phony friends who didn't stick by me when I had some trouble."

"Your friends may not have been there for you, but sounds like your wife stuck by you."

Damon laughed grimly and said sarcastically, "Yeah, it was truly a marriage made in heaven. My wife did move here with me, but I always figured she felt like she had to. Kind of a guilt thing from a long time ago, which I don't want to go into. Sorry she was murdered, but after the last year or so, can't say I'm sorry to see her go."

Just then the player at bat for the Giants hit a grand slam home run, and the bar crowd erupted in screaming and cheering. Roger leaned over to Damon and said, "We've got to go. Nice talking to you and again, sorry about your loss." He motioned to Liz that they were going to leave. Winston followed his lead, stood up, and the three of them walked out of the bar.

When they were in the car a few minutes later, Roger said, "I think we can take Damon off of the suspect list. Sounds like he's got a solid alibi, and Nic will back him up."

"I don't know how reliable a witness Nic would make, but yes, I agree with you. For the time being, we're going to have to look elsewhere. Do you think Nic will notice that I never took a drink of my beer?" she asked.

"I imagine Damon noticed, and he's probably already slid it over in front of him and exchanged it with his empty beer mug. What a sad life when your only enjoyment is going to a neighborhood bar and getting wasted every night. Glad I have you and Winston."

"I'm glad you do, too, and Roger you have to admit, the certificate for Winston was perfect. I'm so glad I got it."

"I'll admit it worked well in a bar. We'll see how it works in a tasting room at a prestigious winery. The jury's still out on whether or not it's a good thing to use, but keep it handy, just in case," he said as he pulled onto the freeway and headed in the direction of Calistoga.

CHAPTER TWENTY

An hour and a half later Roger drove into the parking lot of the Red Stallion Winery. A sign in front of the low-slung building featured a roan colored stallion rearing up on its back legs. Roger and Liz recognized the sign as the same design that had been on the wine label for the cabernet sauvignon the vineyard produced, and which Judy had served the evening before.

"Okay, sweetheart. It's late Saturday afternoon in the summer, so I'm not surprised there are so many cars in the parking lot, to say nothing of the limousines. I'm not sure your certificate ruse will work here, but feel free to try it. I would like Winston with us, if at all possible. I wonder if we'll be able to meet the man who offered to buy Judy's property."

"Judy told me she was under the impression that the man and his wife run the tasting room themselves, because the wine production here is so limited. Even though the wine is very pricey, since they bottle so little, they can't afford a large staff. Why don't you give me Winston's leash, since I'm the anxious one, okay?"

"Here you go," he said handing it to her as he opened the door of the tasting room. The large room was paneled with oak wood, the same type of wood that the wine barrels were made from. Behind the bar was a large oil painting of a red stallion similar to the one that was on the sign outside the door and on the wine labels. There were a number of people standing at a long bar with wine glasses in front of them.

"Welcome to the Red Stallion Winery," a large man said, his grey hair neatly tied at the nape of his neck in a ponytail. "Me and my wife, Winnie, are the owners. Name's Mac Owens. That's Winnie down at the end of the bar. Nice lookin' dog you have there. We're a dog friendly winery, so he's welcome in here as long as he doesn't create a problem."

"He won't. I can guarantee that," Roger said, as he and Liz walked over to the bar.

"You folks been here before?" the man asked.

"We've been in the area, but we had some of your cabernet wine last night and thought we'd see if we could get a bottle of it as long as we were here. It was really, really good."

"Thanks, but I'm sold out of it. I'm closing the wine tasting room beginning next week. I held back enough bottles for tasting to get people interested for next year. The only thing we produce is the cabernet sauvignon. I guess we're doing something right, because we always sell out and win prizes for it."

As Roger was talking to Mac, Liz noticed an attractive older woman clearing used wine glasses from the bar, washing and drying them, and welcoming people who continued to enter the room.

"My wife and I would love to try another taste of it. I'm curious, though. Why don't you produce more if it's that popular?" Roger asked as the man poured a small amount of the wine in each of the wine glasses he'd placed in front of them.

"Friend, I'd like to, believe me. My land abuts up to several other vintners, and they're not about to sell me their vineyards. The only way I can grow is to buy that hotel up the road and the land it's on. I've tried to buy it several times, but never had any luck. It's got a new owner, so I'm hoping she'll fall flat on her face and have to sell it. Truth is, just might happen. One of the guests was murdered at the hotel last night, and that sure isn't going to make people be in a hurry to go there."

Mac was speaking in a loud voice as if he deliberately wanted people to overhear the conversation, and it seemed to be working. There were murmurs of "I wouldn't stay there" and "How did that happen?"

Mac was more than happy to answer their questions and said, "Paper said the heat was too high in the sauna, and a woman died from heat stroke. It also said the doors on the sauna were jammed, and she couldn't get out."

Liz looked around the room and realized everyone had stopped what they were doing to listen to him. She knew within a short time there wouldn't be a person in the valley who hadn't heard that a murder had occurred in the sauna at the Serenity Hotel and Spa. It was the first time she'd considered the possibility that Judy might actually have to close the hotel and spa. It made her more determined than ever to find the murderer.

They finished their wine and Roger said, "Thanks. That was just as good as the one we had last night. I wish you luck. Your wine is the best I've ever had."

"Appreciate your kind words. Who knows? Next time you come here I may have expanded. I can't believe the woman who bought that hotel and spa can make a go of it when a person's been murdered on her property. I'll wait a few days, and then I'll make her an offer. I'll bet she'll accept it this time. When the hotel and spa are replaced with vineyards, be willing to bet the murder will only be a distant memory for most people. Anyway, don't like to see anyone get murdered, but fate has a way of stepping in at times. Maybe this is one of them."

Liz was watching Mac's wife, Winnie, who was working behind him and although it was fleeting, she definitely saw a smile pass over the woman's face. She patted her husband on the shoulder when she walked by him.

I wonder why she did that, Liz thought. *It seemed like kind of an odd response to what he was saying. It was almost like she was congratulating him. Could her husband have been the murderer?*

When they got back to their car, Liz turned to Roger and asked "Well, what did you think of the owner and his wife?"

"I thought it was crass of him to announce the murder in such a loud voice so everyone would hear it, but on the other hand, I can understand his frustration at not being able to produce more wine."

"Something bothers me about him, Roger. I kind of had this deep-down feeling that his wife and he did it. You probably didn't see it, but when he was talking about the murder, she actually smiled, even though it was only for a moment. That's not right."

"I completely agree, but none of that would stand up in a court of law. All you really have is a guy who wants to buy the land that's adjacent to his, so he can expand his winemaking business. Nothing else is solid. You'd need a lot stronger evidence than a facial expression you interpreted as a smile when he was talking about someone being murdered. Sorry, Liz, no matter what your instincts are, at the moment this is a dead end."

"I suppose you're right, but I don't think the impact the murder could have on Judy's business had really sunk in on me until he started talking about how bad it would be for her business and some of the customers standing at the bar were nodding and agreeing with him. We've got to do something."

"We took a long look today at two possible suspects, but don't think either one has worked out. I wish I could stay and help you, but I have a trial on Monday, and I need to prepare for it. I'm planning on leaving about noon tomorrow. Afraid you and Winston will be on your own. Liz, I know how much you hate guns, but I'm going to leave mine with you, and I want you to carry it with you from the time I leave. Will you indulge me on this? I really am concerned about you, and yet I know this is something you feel you have to do. I understand that and it just so happens that I agree with you."

"Yes, Roger, I promise, but I just had an idea, kind of a sting thing. What if the guy who owns the Red Stallion was told that because of the publicity from the murder, instead of being a deterrent to business for Judy, the spa and hotel have sold out for the next two months. If it is him, he might want to commit another murder. I don't know exactly how I could do it, but I think it might have some merit. What do you think?"

"I think it's nuts, but in a weird way it might smoke out the murderer if the motive is related to the hotel and spa. I think we both agree that Damon is not a suspect, even though it was pretty clear his marriage to Nikki was dead. Before you do anything with your new theory, let's see if any more suspects come to light. It's only been about twenty-four hours since Nikki was murdered, and I'm sure we don't know everything yet. Would you hold off doing anything for now?"

"Sure. I need to talk to the chief tonight and see if he's found out anything. Maybe his department knows something. Don't worry, Roger, I promise I'll be careful. I'll have your gun with me, plus I have Winston. What could possibly go wrong?"

"I'd like to say nothing, but that probably wouldn't be realistic. To change the subject, I think you said Judy was fixing pheasant for dinner tonight. Would I be right?"

"That you would. I don't think I've ever served it, and I've only had it occasionally."

"It's one of my favorites. There was a restaurant in San Francisco that specialized in it, and I used to go there about once a month. I don't think I've had pheasant since I left the area."

"Roger, I don't want you to get your hopes up. Cooking is not Judy's forte, although she swears she does a great job with pheasant. Even if it's lousy, tell her how good it is, please, for me?"

"I hope she knows what a good friend she has in you," he said grinning. "You're a very special lady."

"Well, this very special lady has a dog who needs to take a walk and then I'm going to take a quick shower and get the smell of Nic's off of me. I don't think the floor in that sleazy bar has been cleaned in years, and the reason I didn't even taste my beer was that I was afraid the glass had been whisked through water that was probably cold. Yuck!"

CHAPTER TWENTY-ONE

Liz had just finished getting dressed when the phone in their suite rang. Roger answered it and said, "We'll see you then and Judy, I'm really looking forward to it. When Liz told me we were having pheasant for dinner, that made my day."

"When does she want us down there?" Liz asked.

"In half an hour, which is perfect. I'll take Winston for a walk and feed him. He has to be about the easiest dog in the world to travel with. Give him a little food and water, and he's fine."

"That may be true, but I rather doubt too many dogs are staying in suites like this one. It's not too hard to be on your best behavior with accommodations like this."

"You're probably right. Back in a few minutes."

While they were gone, Liz looked at the piece of paper she'd made notes on earlier in the day. She crossed off Damon's name and put a check mark next to Mac's name.

That's two of the people we identified, but there must be more. Roger said he had a funny feeling about Amber. I'll see if I can talk to her tomorrow. Maybe I should talk to Renee first. Yes, that's what I'll do. We still haven't determined if there is anyone else in Calistoga or the surrounding area that might not want

Judy's hotel and spa to make a go of it. It would probably be a good idea for me to look at that angle.

She booted up her laptop and typed in the words 'spas Calistoga, California.' She glanced at the names and quickly counted over twenty-five. She remembered Judy telling her that Calistoga was famous for its natural hot springs. People came from all over the United States to take the "baths." The wealthy people of San Francisco and Los Angeles didn't want to take the "baths" with the commoners, so exclusive spas had been built over the years to accommodate them, many of which were still in business.

Judy's was just one of many. It seemed strange that with so many spas and hotels in the area, a new one would present much competition. Thinking along those lines the only ones who might be affected by the Serenity Hotel and Spa would either be the ones closest to it or other similar high end spas and hotels. Judy had spared no expense on either the spa or the hotel, and it had to be one of the upper end ones. Liz spent the next few minutes jotting down the names of several of them, determined to check them out tomorrow.

She heard Roger and Winston coming down the hall and opened the door for them. "Well, how was the walk?"

"Very nice. Judy's property is beautiful, and she's spared no expense on anything, from the hotel to the spa to the grounds. I can't believe this won't become a destination hotel and spa."

"I hope you're right Roger, but I'm worried. What I don't understand is why someone would consider her to be competition, and while I know we haven't established that as a possible motive, it's certainly a viable theory. While you were gone, I spent some time looking at spas in the area, and there are really a lot of them, and several seem to be very high-end."

"Liz, you know as well as I do that people are strange. While it seems like there would be more than enough business for all the spas, maybe that's not the reality. Maybe there aren't enough spa visitors and several are hurting financially. Maybe another spa thinks Serenity will take some business away from it. I don't know, but I think it should be looked at as a possible motive."

"I'm planning on doing that after you leave tomorrow. It seems to me if a spa is quite some distance from here, it wouldn't be affected very much by Judy opening hers, but if one is closer to Judy's it might be adversely affected. I know we're grasping at straws, but right now, that's about the best I can do."

"Time to meet Judy, and I hope the pheasant is half as good as I remember it being in San Francisco. It doesn't even have to be as good. I'll be satisfied with half."

"For your sake, I hope it is, but I wouldn't bet on it."

CHAPTER TWENTY-TWO

"I'm in the living room," Judy called out as they walked down the hall. "I thought we could start with some cheese and crackers, plus I can't wait to hear what you found out today."

"Judy, this is Red Stallion wine. I understand they're sold out of this year's supply. How did you get a bottle? I know you said the bottle we had last night came from your neighbor, but we finished that one," Roger said.

"My friendly neighbor," she said sarcastically, "showed up on my doorstep about an hour ago with this bottle and made another offer to buy me out. I can't even believe the gall of the man. As insincere as he is, I think it would be hard for him to look in the mirror without cowering in shame. Honestly, you should have heard him."

"What did he say?" Liz asked as she spread warm brie cheese on a cracker. "By the way, Judy, I like this warm brie baked in dough."

"Thanks, I'd like to take credit for it, but Mary made it before she left for the day. All I had to do was put it in the oven, but don't get concerned about dinner. I did make the pheasant all by myself and it's cooking now, however, in full disclosure I have to tell you she made the salad and did all the prep work for the noodles as well as the mushroom green bean quick fry."

"We're really looking forward to it, particularly Roger. He told me it's one of his favorite meals, and he said there used to be a restaurant in San Francisco that specialized in it. He told me he went there all the time when he lived in San Francisco. Now, let's hear what happened with your neighbor."

"The guy is just a smarmy toad. He told me how sorry he was to hear about the little problem that had taken place in the sauna. I mean, how many people call a murder a little problem? Then he went on to tell me he was sure I would want to sell the hotel and spa, since the murder would adversely affect my business. He said that the longer I held out the lower the price would be that anyone would offer me, and he suggested I rethink my numerous turndowns."

"I hate to agree with him, Judy," Roger said, "but there is some truth to what he's saying. If, for some reason, the murderer is not found, there will be a dark cloud hanging over the hotel and spa. I'm sorry, but the fact is you're running a business, a brand-new business, and something has happened that could adversely affect its success."

"It kills me to say it, Roger, but I know you're right. I suppose I have to take my head out of the sand and admit this could ruin my plans for the Serenity Hotel and Spa. I've put so much time and money into it, it just doesn't seem fair."

Liz reached over and put her hand on Judy's. "It's not over yet. The murder only occurred a little more than twenty-four hours ago. I have some ideas on things we can do to catch the killer, so don't get discouraged this soon. Okay?"

"Thanks, Liz. It's just hard not to get depressed about the whole thing when he suggested I rethink his previous offers. I felt like I was fresh roadkill, and he was the vulture who was ready to feed off of me. Believe me, it didn't make me feel very good."

"I'm sure it didn't. Judy, I'm smelling pheasant. Maybe it's time to eat? We can tell you what happened this afternoon over dinner."

Judy looked at her watch and said, "It's definitely time to eat. If we stay here any longer, we'll be eating very tough pheasant for dinner, and I'm sure you don't want to do that, Roger." She hurried towards the kitchen and said over her shoulder, "Meet me in the dining room. I'll plate it in the kitchen and bring it in to you."

Roger looked at Liz who shrugged her shoulders in an "I told you so" gesture.

An hour later Roger said, "Judy, that pheasant is just as good as what I used to have in San Francisco. If you don't mind, I think I'll go in the kitchen and have seconds, and Liz, I'd really like you to get the recipe. If this keeps up, we'll have to publish a Serenity Hotel Cookbook."

"Liz, I'm glad Nikki's husband has an alibi for where he was at the time of her death. I'd hate to think her husband was the murderer, although it probably would have been better for my business. It could be explained as a domestic dispute that got out of hand rather than a vendetta against a new business."

"I had the sense that Damon's life was not a happy one. I told you what his neighbor said about them fighting and Nikki staying with him because he'd married her when she was pregnant."

"Maybe she still loved him, even with everything that happened over the last few years. Remember all the political wives we've seen on television standing next to their husbands when the media got wind of the men having affairs or worse. All of those women stayed with their husbands, and I think it's kind of a generational thing. Women today don't feel they have to stay in a bad marriage anymore, because they have careers of their own. Women of Nikki's age aren't quite that independent, and that may have been part of it, but we'll never know. I just think the whole thing is so sad."

"Success," Roger said as he walked back into the dining room. "I found several more pieces of pheasant, and since I was sure neither one of you would want to risk ruining your fabulous figures, I decided I would take the temptation away from you. Actually, it was quite a sacrifice on my part, but that's the kind of man I am, someone who doesn't want you to hear the seductive voice of the rest of the pheasant calling to you."

"Roger, that's a stretch even for you, but I guess we'll grudgingly let you enjoy the pheasant," Liz said laughing.

"Not only have you helped us save our girlish figures, you've made Liz respect my cooking abilities," Judy said. "Who knows? Maybe I should get rid of Mary and make breakfast myself."

"Judy, you're my best friend, but let me give you a little advice. One dish does not a chef make. Stick with the pheasant, and let Mary do the rest of the cooking."

Liz had brought her purse into the dining room, because she didn't want to miss Chief Oliphant's call. She'd just finished speaking when her cell phone rang. "Excuse me, but I need to take this call. I'll be back in a few minutes."

CHAPTER TWENTY-THREE

"This is Liz Langley," she said certain that the person calling was the police chief. She was right.

"Good evening, Mrs. Langley. It's Chief Oliphant. How are you?"

"Please, call me Liz, and I'm fine. How's the reunion going?"

"Great. Everyone's here now, and we're getting ready to eat in a few minutes. We're barbecuing steaks, and they're going on the grill as I speak. I'm lucky that I'm able to take and make calls from here. They must have brought in some new equipment. The last time I was here the phone reception was either lousy or non-existent. And my wife says thanks for helping and allowing me to come. She told me if I'd stayed in Calistoga it could have been a deal breaker, and as I think I mentioned, our marriage is a little too new to test that out," he said laughing.

"My pleasure, although it's been a bit of a frustrating day." She told him about going to Sacramento and meeting Damon as well as going to the Red Stallion tasting room. She omitted the part about going to The Dog Spa since that conversation had never existed. "So, Chief, what do you think?"

"I agree with yours and Roger's conclusions. It sounds like Damon didn't have anything to do with his wife's murder, and although we usually start with a spouse, that doesn't seem to be in play here. As far as the owner of the vineyard next door to Mrs. Rasmussen, I don't know what to think.

"It seems a stretch to imagine the owner would commit murder in order to get the property, particularly since he's quite successful in his own right, but people never fail to amaze me. My department did get a call today that may have some bearing on the case."

"What was the call about?"

"A few months ago, Calistoga held a special election to fill an open seat on the city council. The prior councilman had died from pancreatic cancer. Since there aren't any term limits for the council members, it's a prized political position, and a number of people ran. The winner was a man by the name of Jim Michaelson. I supported him privately. As the police chief, I couldn't openly endorse him, but I've known him for years and always found him to be an honest and good person. I was glad when he won."

"I'm listening, but I'm not connecting the dots between someone getting elected to the city council and a woman being murdered."

"I'm getting there, Liz, stay with me. I just need to give you a little background."

"Sorry, Chief."

"No problem. Anyway, my department got a call from Jim today. He wanted to speak with me, but when they told him I was on a short vacation, he spoke with my chief deputy. Jim told him he'd received a telephone call a few weeks earlier from a woman who had supported his campaign financially. She'd read in the paper that the Serenity Hotel and Spa was going to open on July 28th and she was furious. In the excitement of winning the election, he'd forgotten she'd asked him to tell the man he'd appointed to the Calistoga Planning Commission to deny any requested land use variances for the new spa. She didn't want any more competition for her spa."

"I think that could possibly qualify as a motive for murder, don't you?" she asked.

"I don't know if I'd go that far, but I think it bears looking into. I've met the woman. Her name is Simone LaSalle, and she owns La Spa. It's not too far from Mrs. Rasmussen's spa, and it's really a high-end spa. Anyway, when she called Jim she was furious, said he hadn't upheld his end of the bargain, and she'd never support him again. He didn't think much about it at the time, but when he read the paper this morning, he remembered the conversation and thought he should tell me."

"Sounds like an honorable man. What happened with his planning commissioner?"

"He told my deputy that there was so much to learn and do after he won the election, it completely slipped his mind. Jim said it probably would have stayed where it had gone, if he hadn't read the article. He said he wasn't accusing this LaSalle woman or even pointing a finger at her, but it was something he thought I should know."

"I agree. I was planning on visiting some spas in the area tomorrow. So far we've gotten nowhere looking at the murder being about Nikki. I'd like to look at it from the angle of the Serenity Hotel and Spa. I'll make an appointment for a treatment tomorrow at La Spa, and see if I can find out anything. There is one other thing I want to clear up. Roger feels that Amber Ruiz had a strange reaction to Nikki's murder, and if you remember, Renee told Judy that she had wondered if Amber was jealous of Nikki. Renee didn't seem to know why, but given what's happened, I suppose nothing should be overlooked."

"You might want to talk to both Renee and Amber and see if you can learn anything."

"I'm planning on doing that. Looks like I'll have a full day tomorrow, and Roger is leaving around noon, so I'll call La Spa in the morning and see if I can get an afternoon appointment. I imagine

Sunday is a busy day for spas in this area since a lot of people probably decide to take advantage of the spas and healing waters before they leave the area and head for home."

"It looks like they're taking the steaks off the barbecue, Liz, and I don't have anything else to tell you. Be careful, keep that dog with you, and I'll call you tomorrow night. Good luck."

"Thanks, and have a wonderful time with your family."

Liz walked back into the dining room and sat down at the table while Roger and Judy looked at her expectantly. "Well," Roger said, "what did the chief have to say?"

She told them about her conversation with him and about the call his department had received from Jim Michaelson regarding Simone LaSalle, the owner of La Spa. Liz turned to Judy and said, "Have you met her?"

"No. There's a group of spa owners who meet monthly to share information, things like where to get certain products, etc. I remember her name because someone mentioned that Simone would never attend their meetings and share information, but if one of them happened to see her in town, she had no compunctions about finding out what she could from them. I gather she wasn't very well liked."

"I'm going to see if I can have a treatment there tomorrow afternoon. I don't know what I'm looking for, but maybe I can find out something."

They heard the front door open and the sound of feminine voices. "We're in the dining room," Judy said.

A moment later Renee, Amber, Tiffany, and Nancy walked into the room. "How was dinner?" Judy asked.

"As good as you'd said it would be. Simply wonderful. Actually, it was some of the best Italian food I've ever had. I'd be tempted to eat there tomorrow evening on our way out of town, but I've already made reservations for us in San Francisco at a French restaurant that's one of my favorites. I wish we could stay here longer, but Tiffany has to get back to work, and this is about the normal length of our reunions, although we did spend a little more time in France, simply because it didn't make sense to go all the way there for just a few days."

"Renee, Judy, everyone, I'm completely relaxed from my spa treatments and dinner. Please excuse me, but I'm going to bed," Tiffany said. "Anyone else coming up with me?" Amber and Nancy followed her out the door.

"Judy, were you able to find out anything today regarding Nikki's murder?" Renee asked. Judy nodded to Liz who told her about their conversation with Damon, the wine tasting room, and her recent conversation with the chief. Liz ended by saying, "I can see that you're tired, and this must be a terrible strain on you, but I would like to talk to you. I have a couple of questions. Could you meet me for breakfast tomorrow morning?"

"Yes, that would be fine. My first spa treatment isn't until 10:00 in the morning, so why don't we meet here for breakfast at 8:00. Would that be all right with you?"

"Yes. Go to bed, and I'll see you then."

"Okay, see you then." Renee said as she left the dining room. Liz turned to Roger and said, "Sorry to abandon you for breakfast, but I might be able to find out more by myself instead of both of us questioning her."

"That's fine. As a matter of fact, I talked to Judy earlier today about the possibility of getting a massage treatment before I leave tomorrow. She asked her massage therapist if she could fit me in, and she said she'd be happy to, so I'll be having my spa treatment while you talk to Renee. With that, I think we need to go to bed as well. While we didn't solve the murder today, it's still been an intense day. Winston, come, let's take one last trip outside."

CHAPTER TWENTY-FOUR

"Enjoy your massage," Liz said the next morning as Roger left the room in a fluffy white bathrobe and slippers. "By the way, if any of your downtown San Francisco friends see you in that robe and slippers, your reputation may take a beating."

"Thanks, Liz. For that you can take Winston outside this morning. See you later."

"Come on, Winston, let's commune with nature." A few minutes later she and Winston walked back into their suite from the private door that led to the back yard and she fed him in the bathroom, so if he sloshed any of his dog food onto the floor it wouldn't hurt the Oriental rugs that Judy had carefully chosen for the suite. She knew from experience that tile was a lot easier to clean.

She opened the door to the hallway, and as he'd been trained to do, Winston followed her down the hall. Liz walked into the dining room where Renee was sitting at a table in the corner drinking a cup of coffee.

"Good morning, Renee. Thanks for meeting me this early, although you look as if you've been up for hours."

"I've gotten into the habit of taking an early morning walk, and since my house is located very close to the financial district in San Francisco, I almost always run into someone I know. I've learned it's a lot easier to get up a little earlier and take care of my makeup and hair, than regret not having done it when I meet someone unexpectedly. I noticed your dog yesterday. I'm a dog lover, but my small yard isn't large enough for that breed. May I pet him?"

"Of course, as long as I say it's okay, he's very friendly, but he's also a very good guard dog. My husband insists I have him with me all the time."

"I have three small dogs, and they make up for their lack of brawn with their bark. I've always felt safe with them in the house."

"Excuse me, Mrs. Langley, may I bring you some coffee or juice this morning?" Nettie asked.

"Just a cup of coffee, thank you." Nettie left the table to get the coffee and Liz said, "Renee, I really appreciate you meeting me. I wanted to talk to you about Amber. Judy mentioned to me that you told her you'd always wondered if Amber was jealous of Nikki, and my husband said that Amber didn't seem as shocked or upset as the others when he sat in on the statements they gave Chief Oliphant. Can you tell me anything about that?" She smiled up at Nettie as she placed a cup of coffee in front of Liz.

"I've been thinking a lot about that over the last couple of days. We were college roommates so long ago that I'm sure my thinking is somewhat fuzzy regarding everything that took place during that time."

"I can understand that. My thinking gets fuzzy sometimes when I try to remember what I did yesterday," Liz said laughing. "Guess that's one of those things that happens as we get older, but whatever you can remember might help Judy, and I know what good friends you are with her."

"Yes, I just wish I could do more for her. I thought it would help her opening weekend to have the reunion here, but the way it's turned out, it may have just the opposite effect."

"You can't blame yourself. You had no way of knowing

something like this would happen."

"Intellectually, I know that. Emotionally, I'm having a hard time with it. I keep thinking if we hadn't come here this weekend, in time this hotel and spa definitely would have been successful and now, because of everything that's happened, it's questionable whether that can happen. Okay, back to Amber. I assume Judy told you how she got to Berkeley, so I don't need to go over that again.

"Tiffany, Nancy, Nikki, and I had pretty much been raised by parents of means. I'm sure Judy told you my story, and I probably have more means than most. I'm not telling you that to boast, but it's simply a fact. Amber was from a whole different world. From the little I know her parents were very poor, and the only way she was able to get a college degree was because of a scholarship. She's a very smart woman."

"Does she work now? I seem to remember something about her husband owning a farm. What do you know about that?" Liz asked.

Renee was quiet for a few moments as she thought while she drank her coffee. She put the cup down and said, "Yes, he owns a farm, but I don't think it's very big or very successful. Liz, I really don't like to gossip, and this is close to it, but if this will help Judy in any way, I'll tell you something I've never shared with anyone. Nikki didn't like Amber, and I think Amber sensed it. Nikki was not a very charitable person. She felt she was above most people because of her parent's wealth and the fact they lived in a very exclusive enclave in Hillsborough."

"Renee, Judy found out what happened to Nikki's husband and why they had to leave San Francisco. Roger and I went to Sacramento and talked to him. I don't like to gossip either, but you probably need to know this to flesh out the picture." Liz told her about their conversation with the neighbor and Damon.

Renee looked at Liz with a stricken look on her face. "This is almost like some horrible karma. I remember one time Nikki told me she didn't like Amber's boyfriend coming over to our apartment because he was beneath us. She also said Amber didn't have any manners and didn't even know how to properly hold a knife and fork.

"I always wondered if Amber overheard that conversation. I've played it in my mind a million times since then, and I clearly remember telling Nikki I didn't want to hear any more talk like that. A few moments later Amber walked in and said her class had been cancelled. Maybe we didn't hear her open the door the first time, and she loudly opened it the second time, so we'd be aware she'd returned."

"Renee, I'm sorry to ask you this, but do you think Amber is capable of murder? Did you ever get a sense that she hated Nikki? Do you think she knew about Nikki's husband? And something else I've wondered about. Since she and her husband seem to be just eking out a living on their farm, how can she justify the expense involved with these reunions? I would think she wouldn't want anything to do with people who are obviously successful."

"I'll try to answer your questions as best I can. No, I don't think Amber is capable of murder, but then again, I don't understand how anyone can murder another human being unless it's in self-defense. I struggle with the death penalty. I don't have the killing gene in me, that I know. Did she hate Nikki? Maybe she did if she overheard that conversation I told you about, but I don't know."

"I, too, have a hard time understanding how anyone can kill another human being," Liz said.

"I think Amber justifies the reunions, maybe not consciously, but subconsciously, as a way to escape what her life has become," Renee said. "Let's face it, she came from poverty, and it looks like she's close to poverty again, but for a few days she gets to relive the time when she was free from it. Her scholarship provided the funds for her to live in a nice apartment with other women who were not impoverished. It many ways it was probably the best time of her life."

"That makes perfect sense, Renee. I wonder what her husband

thinks about it."

"I haven't seen Daniel since we were in college, but my memory of him is that he was really a nice man. He always treated Amber well, and I know he loved her very much. Since they're still together and she comes to these reunions, I would think she has his blessing to do so."

"One last question, Renee, and then we probably should get something to eat before your spa appointment. Do you think you'll continue having these reunions now that Nikki's dead?"

"I have a feeling we won't. We talked about that at dinner last night, and from the sense I got, this will probably be the last one. Ironically, the next person up to plan the reunion is Amber, and last night she made the comment that maybe the time had come to stop having them. Tiffany said that it would probably be hard for us to meet and not think about Nikki being murdered. I would imagine that there won't be any more of them. I guess all things have to come to an end, and this is one of them."

"Thanks, Renee. I really appreciate you taking the time to talk to me. I don't know what I'll be able to do with this information, if anything, but it can't hurt. All this talking has made me hungry, and Mary is a very good cook. Let's eat."

CHAPTER TWENTY-FIVE

"Liz, are you sure you'll be okay here? Maybe I should call the court and tell them I'm sick. I could stay here a couple more days and by then Chief Oliphant will have returned from his vacation and he can take over."

"Absolutely not. I have Winston and you've given me your gun, although I'm sure I won't be needing it, but trust me, we'll be fine. I made a spa appointment at La Spa for 2:00 this afternoon. I'll call you tonight and tell you how that goes. It should be interesting. I looked up the owner on the Internet. She's French and imports all of her spa products from France. Since I've never been to France, I'm probably in for a treat."

"Liz, I know how bizarre this is going to sound, but I know you like to make me happy, don't you?"

"Of course I do. Why do you even need to ask?"

"Well, I'd like you to take Winston with you and keep him in the room with you when you have your spa treatment."

"You're right, that does sound bizarre. What will the massage therapist think when I tell her I want my dog to stay in the room?"

"You can tell her pretty much what you told Nic about you

needing a comfort dog, and you could even show her the certificate from your doctor."

"Right, and she'd probably think I was a bona fide nut case. She may even refuse to give me a treatment."

"Liz, you forget that money talks. I'd bet she'd say it was just fine with her. Anyway, would you try it for me?"

"Roger, you're a little too old to try and pull off that puppy dog look you're giving me. I think little kids who are about five or six can get away with it, but it looks ridiculous on a grown man."

"You're probably right. I won't try that again. Okay, I'll just ask it up front. Liz, I'd appreciate it if you'd take Winston with you when you have your spa treatment today."

"Why, Roger, I'd be happy to. See how easy that was?"

"Don't push it, Liz. I love you, and I just don't want anything to happen to you." he said bending down to kiss her as he was getting into Judy's Mercedes.

"Okay. I do have to say you look pretty good driving that Mercedes of Judy's. One thing she has is very good taste, but don't get used to it. Talk to you tonight," she said waving to him as he drove down the lane to the street.

A few minutes before 2:00 Liz left the hotel and followed the instructions on her GPS to La Spa. She turned down a long driveway that ended in a horseshoe in front of a building that had been designed to resemble a French chateau and parked in a slot with a sign indicating it was for guests. She sat in the car for a moment looking at the building.

Simone LaSalle must have come to the United States with a lot of money. This is the one of the most beautiful buildings I've ever seen. It looks like whoever built it spent a lot of time studying French chateau architecture, because it sure looks like buildings I've seen in books and on television.

I probably should have asked how much my treatment is going to cost, although with the number of treatment rooms that this building could accommodate, she probably makes her money from doing a large volume of treatments. I might understand it if she was concerned about competition from Serenity Spa cutting into her profits. Based on the size of La Spa, it looks like it would take a lot of appointments to simply make ends meet, much less a profit, but maybe that's not a concern of hers.

She put Winston's leash on him and opened the door that had a sign on it with the words "Please Come In" formed with brass letters. She walked over to the reception desk and said, "Hi, my name is Liz Langley, and I have a two o'clock appointment for a massage."

"Welcome to La Spa," a beautiful young woman with a heavy French accent said. "I'm sorry, but we don't allow dogs in here, because some of our clients are allergic to them."

"I understand, but I have a note from my doctor with me. I suffer from anxiety, and my dog is a comfort dog. He goes everywhere with me. He's perfectly trained."

The young woman looked skeptically at Liz for a moment and then at Winston. "I will need to call your therapist and make sure she's not allergic to dogs."

"Thank you, I'd appreciate that."

A moment later the young woman looked up at Liz and said, "It's highly unusual, but Antoinette said that would be fine, because she likes dogs. Let me show you to the changing rooms. Please follow me."

A few minutes later Liz was wearing a bathrobe very similar to the one Roger had worn that morning along with spa slippers. She put her purse in the locker that had been assigned to her, turned the key, and walked out to the reception desk.

"Go through that door, and you can relax in there. Antoinette will come and escort you to her treatment room in a few minutes. There is tea and other refreshments in the room. Please help yourself."

Liz and Winston walked through the door, and as she looked out the window, she saw that the chateau had been designed around a central courtyard where the guests could enjoy the jacuzzi. Recliners covered in soft white velour were scattered throughout the room while gentle music created a peaceful feeling. Even though it was late July, a fire had been lit and candles glowed throughout the room. Large cut glass pitchers held three kinds of water, one with sliced cucumbers, one with sliced oranges, and one with sliced limes. A tray of petits fours had been carefully arranged and set on the counter along with a variety of teas and an urn with hot water. A great attention to detail was evident everywhere she looked.

She sat down in one of the recliners with a magazine and felt the tension she'd been carrying with her ever since she and Roger had arrived at Judy's slowly leave her body. A few moments later a petite woman with large brown eyes and black hair framing her face said, "You must be Mrs. Langley. My name is Antoinette. I'll be your masseuse today. Please follow me, and I understand that this dog will be accompanying you, which is fine with me. When I left France, I couldn't bring mine with me, and I still miss him."

Liz followed her down a long hall and up a flight of stairs. "Have you been in the United States for very long?" she asked.

Antoinette opened the door to a large dimly lit room which smelled of sandalwood and said, "What you smell is sandalwood. It has a lot of healing properties in it, and I use essential oils such as sandalwood in my massages. I think you'll like it. To answer your question, I've been here for two years. Madame LaSalle travels to France every year and hires several people trained in different beauty and spa techniques to work here at La Spa. She wants to retain the French feeling and felt if she hired Americans, she would lose it."

"That makes sense. This room is one of the most calming rooms I've ever been in. I notice you even have a fountain in the corner. That's a wonderful touch, and I love the walls covered in the French provincial blue fabric. You've done a beautiful job decorating the room."

"Thank you, but I can't take credit for it. Madame LaSalle oversees everything. I'm going to leave you for a few moments. Please take your robe off. There's a hook on the back of the door. You can lie face down on the massage table and cover yourself with the light blanket which has been warmed for you. If you'd like a drink of water before I begin, there's some water with sliced limes in it on the bureau." She opened the door and walked out.

Liz looked around and couldn't believe the amount of money that had obviously been spent on the treatment room. *I thought the Red Cedar Spa was done beautifully, but this takes spa treatments to a different level. Madame LaSalle must have an unlimited amount of money to spend.*

She made herself comfortable on the table, and shortly there was a knock on the door. Antoinette said, "Are you ready for me to come in?"

"Yes, thank you."

"I will start with your shoulders and neck and work my way down. When I have finished with your back side, I will ask you to turn over and do your legs, feet, shoulders and arms. Do you have any questions before I begin?"

"Not about the treatment, but I am curious about the person who owns this spa. Can you tell me something about her?" Liz asked as Antoinette began to work on her neck and upper back.

"The woman who owns La Spa is Simone LaSalle. She married an American who had been assigned to the Paris office of an international banking firm. When his term was over, she moved to San Francisco with him, but the marriage didn't work out. She had been to Calistoga several times and decided it needed an upper-end spa which she had built in the manner of a French chateau. I don't think she's left one detail undone," she said as she began to gently knead the muscles in Liz's mid-back.

"This is my first spa experience in Calistoga. Are all the spas as luxurious as this one?"

Antoinette laughed. "Non, this is very special. Madame spares no expense. She is from one of the wealthiest families in Provence, you know, southern France. Her family owns the largest vineyard and olive oil company in France. That's why she liked Calistoga and decided to settle here, because it reminded her of Provence."

"I've not been to France, but when I entered La Spa, I felt like I was there."

"That is exactly how she wants the clients to feel. There is no other spa like this one in all of the Napa Valley."

"I heard that a new spa just opened. I think it's called the Serenity Spa or something," Liz said.

"Yes, Veronique, she's one of the other massage therapists here, told me that Madame was very, very angry when she heard it was going to open. She told Veronique that she would personally make sure that Serenity Spa wouldn't be open very long, and we didn't need to worry about it. She said she had her ways."

"That's a strange thing to say. What do you think she meant by that?" Liz asked.

"I don't know, but when she says something, you can plan on it happening or not happening. It's too bad that Serenity probably won't be in business for long. Madame will see to it one way or another. Now we've talked long enough, and I want you to simply lie there and let me do the work. By the way, your dog is very well-behaved. He's just lying under the table. He makes me miss mine all the more."

"What kind of dog did you have?" Liz asked.

"I will answer that question, and then nothing more. I had a French poodle, but what would you expect?" Antoinette answered laughing.

An hour later she said, "I am finished. You may stay here for a few minutes, and when you're ready, feel free to spend some time in the lounge or in the jacuzzi if you'd like. We do ask that you shower before you go in the jacuzzi, so as not to get the sandalwood oil I used on you in the jacuzzi. Adieu," she said as she left the room.

CHAPTER TWENTY-SIX

It was late afternoon by the time Liz returned to the Serenity Hotel. She'd thought about what Antoinette had said about Madame LaSalle on her drive back, and wondered how far the woman was willing to go to ensure that Serenity didn't make it. It was hard to believe she might be responsible for Nikki's murder, but it was just as hard for her to believe that the owner of the Red Stallion Winery would commit murder just to get land.

She parked her car and took Winston for a walk. When she returned to the hotel she saw Amber relaxing by the pool. She'd wanted to talk to her and see if she could learn anything from her.

"Winston, you haven't explored the grass by the pool yet, and I think this a perfect time to do it." They walked through the gate and over to where Amber was reading a book and reclining on a chaise longue. She looked up when she heard Liz's footsteps on the concrete apron of the pool.

"Hello, Amber. Mind if we join you? It's such a beautiful afternoon I'm not quite ready to go inside for the rest of the day."

"Please join me. The others are taking a nap before we head back to San Francisco, but I wanted to soak up a little more sun. I don't have many chances to relax like this."

"Amber, I seem to remember that you live down in the Central Valley. Doesn't it get pretty hot there this time of year?" Liz asked, not sure how she was going to lead up to Nikki's murder and not sure what she was looking for.

"Yes, it's brutal, particularly now that the air conditioning unit in our house isn't working. Our farm isn't doing very well, so we can't afford to get it fixed right now. You're probably aware of the drought here in California. It's really hurt our crops, and since the farm isn't doing well we can't afford to hire many workers. It's a pretty rough time right now for farmers."

"Amber, did you live in the Central Valley before you went to college?"

"Yes, I've lived there my whole life other than when I was at Berkeley. I was very lucky to get a scholarship. I really thought I'd go on to graduate school and get a master's degree. I love books, and I always wanted to be an editor, but that didn't happen. I fell in love in high school with my husband-to-be. He also got a scholarship to Berkeley, but he convinced me to marry him and help him run his family's farm. He's a wonderful man, and even though it's not been easy for us, I've never regretted it."

"You're the only one of the reunion people who lives on a farm, aren't you?"

"I am, and it's something Nikki never let me forget."

"What do you mean?"

"I shouldn't speak ill of the dead, but now that she's gone, it probably doesn't matter. Nikki felt I was beneath her and the others who shared the apartment we lived in at Berkeley. I never told any of them, but when they weren't around she said things to me like I had no manners, and that Daniel shouldn't come to the apartment, because he was just trailer trash and as uncouth as I was. She never said anything when any of the others were there, but Nikki made my life miserable in a million little ways," she said bitterly.

"I'm surprised your roommates didn't pick up on that."

"Renee wouldn't stand for anything like that. In many ways, she seems almost too good to be true. She doesn't gossip or listen to it, and she sure wouldn't have allowed any of us to say something unkind about one of the others. One time I overheard Nikki talking to Renee about me, and believe me, it wasn't very complimentary. Renee stopped her from going any farther. I've never forgotten how wonderful Renee was at that moment and how awful Nikki was."

"If you felt that way, Amber, why did you continue to attend the reunions?"

"To be sure Nikki didn't say anything bad about me. As long as I came to them, she wouldn't be able to. I guess it was a form of self-protection. Now that she's gone, I don't think I'll be attending any more reunions, and quite frankly, I'd be surprised if the other three even hold them. Too many bad memories associated with this one."

"Amber, it must have been difficult for you to be around Nikki all these years. I think I would have had a problem with that."

"It was. I hated her, pure and simple. I'm not sorry she's dead, and I'm not sorry that she's no longer the rich wife of some real estate developer. I didn't have anything to do with either one of those things, but I'm sure not sorry they happened to her. What I am glad about is that I had an ironclad alibi for the time she was murdered. Renee was in my room with me, and she and I were catching up on what our children were doing and things of that nature."

Wish I'd thought to ask Renee about Amber's whereabouts when we talked at breakfast, and I could have done without having this talk.

Just then Renee walked out to the pool and said, "Amber, we'll be leaving in about half an hour. Just wanted to make sure you were packed. Hi, Liz. I hear you had a spa treatment at La Spa, but I want to tell you that the treatments I've had here at Serenity beat any I've had anywhere in the world. Judy has done an incredible job. So, are you two just soaking up the sunshine?"

"We are. Amber was just filling me in on her life. She was telling me that the two of you spent some time when you got here catching up on your children, etc."

"We did. I went in her room right after we arrived here on Friday, and we were there until I remembered that I'd told Nikki I'd meet her in the sauna. Maybe if I'd gone to the sauna earlier, she'd still be alive."

"Renee, we've talked about this before. None of this is your fault. You couldn't have prevented it. Please, don't blame yourself. Who knows? If you had gone to the sauna earlier, you might have suffered the same fate as Nikki."

"I hadn't even thought of that. I guess I was lucky. I know a lot of people believe when it's your time, it's your time. This might make me a believer in that."

Amber and Liz stood up and joined Renee as they walked into the hotel, Winston dutifully following them.

CHAPTER TWENTY-SEVEN

After she left the pool area, Liz decided to stop by Judy's office and see how she was doing. She was in her office sitting behind her desk with a glum expression on her face. "Hi, Judy, what's the problem?" Liz asked.

"I had all the rooms rented for next weekend and two of them just cancelled. One of them said her husband had to go out of town on business, and the other one said she was having unexpected houseguests. I'd be willing to bet neither one of those stories is true, and they're cancelling because they heard about Nikki's murder. Liz, this really could wipe me out. I've put almost all the money I have into this. I'm getting really, really scared."

"I know you can't help worrying, but we'll come up with something. I'll make you a proposition. Let's eat here tonight. I'll see what you have in the kitchen, and I'll cook for us. As for the murder, two heads are better than one, and I want to tell you about my experience at La Spa. It was interesting. Let's meet in the living room in two hours. I need to make some notes. Okay with you?"

"Sounds great. Anyway, I think I'm too depressed to go out to eat. Renee and her group will be leaving shortly, and I need to say goodbye to them. How do you say goodbye and it was wonderful meeting you when one of their group was murdered in your sauna?"

"Fortunately, I'm sure you'll never have to go through this again. I had a conversation with Amber this afternoon, and from what I learned evidently Nikki wasn't quite the nice person people thought she was. I wouldn't be too surprised if in their heart of hearts, the reunion attendees didn't know that. See you in living room at let's say, 6:30. Okay?"

"Yes. Thanks for doing this, Liz. I really appreciate it."

"Come on, Winston. Let's see what we can come up with for dinner tonight," she said as they walked toward the kitchen. She spent some time finding out what was available in the pantry, refrigerator, and freezer. She saw some chicken breasts and put them in the microwave to defrost, not quite sure how she was going to fix them, but figured that was a good start.

Hmm, I could sauté these chicken breasts in some olive oil and when they're browned, I could put some mushrooms, green onions, and garlic in the pan and lightly sauté those. While that's cooking, I'll make a white sauce and pour it over the chicken and the vegetables. There's also quite a bit of rice left from last night. I can serve the chicken over that. I saw some frozen biscuits and along with a salad, that should be plenty. There's still some cheese and crackers from the other night. That's more than enough for the two of us.

She did the prep work, assembled the chicken dish, prepared the salad, and set the table. When she had almost finished, she heard Judy saying goodbye to Renee and her group. She walked into the front hall where Renee's driver was picking up their luggage and putting it in the large trunk of the limousine.

"I didn't want you to leave without saying goodbye," Liz said. "I'm glad I had a chance to meet all of you, but I'm sorry it was under these circumstances. If you ever decide to do another reunion, I'd love for you to come to the Red Cedar Spa. Have a safe drive back to the San Francisco." She waved goodbye and walked down the hall to her suite. An idea had been forming in her mind, and she wanted to jot down some notes before she met Judy for dinner.

She walked into the kitchen at 6:00, started the oven, then put the chicken into the oven after she'd made the sauce. Liz took the cheese and crackers into the living room and opened a bottle of white wine she'd found in the wine refrigerator. A few minutes later Judy walked into the room and said, "This looks wonderful. I could use a little downtime. What did you think of La Spa? Did you meet Simone LaSalle?"

"No, but first here's a glass of wine and a plate for the cheese and crackers. It's been a very interesting day." She told her about her conversations with Renee, Antoinette, and Amber. "Judy, I made a bunch of notes. Let me use you as a sounding board. I'm not exactly sure where I'm going with this, but I'd like to run it by you and see what you think. If you feel it's too bizarre, I won't go any farther with it." She spent the next half hour outlining some thoughts she had.

When she was finished, she looked at her watch and said, "Dinner's ready. We can talk some more while we're eating."

A few minutes later Judy said, "Liz, this is delicious. Did you bring the recipe with you?"

"No, it comes from years of cooking. You kind of learn what goes well with what. I thought it would work, and I'm happy to say I think it did." She continued, "Judy, as you can tell from the loose plan I outlined to you, I don't think Nikki's death had anything to do with her personally. I believe it really was a case of being in the wrong place at the wrong time. Whoever was in the sauna at that time would have died. She was literally an innocent victim, and the reason I say that is her husband and Amber have pretty rock solid alibis."

Judy put her fork down and looked at Liz. "You really think this happened because someone wants my spa to be unsuccessful, don't you? And from what you told me, Simone doesn't want to see it become successful, because she's afraid it would affect her spa adversely. Mac doesn't want me to be successful because he wants to get my land, so he can turn the land into more vineyards. It's nothing personal against me, it's economics. Does that about sum it up?"

"Yes. That definitely is what I think. So, we need you to be successful or at least for them to think you're successful. Do you see what I've been getting at?"

"It's kind of like a sting you'd see in some movie or on television. What makes you think it would work?" Judy asked in an excited voice.

"I think Simone's reasons for wanting to see you fail is based on her ego. I've not met her, but La Spa is a testimony to opulence and good taste. If her spa became unsuccessful, I think she has so much of her ego wrapped up in it, she would do about anything to keep it from being anything less than what it is. From what I understand from Antoinette, it's kind of the premiere one around here, and Serenity represents a real threat to her.

"Mac's ego is at stake here too. His wine is the best in the valley for now, but how long can he continue to produce award winning wines? I did some research on the Internet today and found out that his cousin is his viticulturist, and he oversees the winemaking at Red Stallion Winery. I don't think it's much of a stretch to say that someone who's responsible for making award-winning wine would be highly in demand in a region known throughout the world for its wine. I'd even think he could probably ask and get whatever salary he wanted, and I'd bet some of the larger wineries would pay whatever he asked to have him work for them. Blood matters, but money talks. In other words, Mac's viticulturist, his cousin, is getting too big of a reputation for Mac to afford him with the rather small winery he presently has.

"If his cousin left, it would probably mean that the caliber of the wine would diminish as would Mac's reputation as a premier winemaker. So, while ego plays a part in his motive, it could also be fueled by economics. At some point, he'll be unable to afford his viticulturist who will leave to go with one of the big wineries. Human nature being what it is, I imagine that time isn't too far off."

As she had the night before, she'd put her purse next to her chair when they sat down for dinner. When she heard her cell phone ring, she opened her purse and looked at the monitor. It was the police chief. "Hello, Chief. Excuse me for just a moment." She turned to Judy and said, "You're heard all this, so I'll go back to my suite and talk to him there. Why don't you take the dishes into the kitchen? I saw some ice cream in the freezer, and that might be a nice way to finish dinner. I'll be back in a few minutes."

CHAPTER TWENTY-EIGHT

"How's the family reunion doing? Everyone still getting along?" Liz laughingly asked the chief.

"Better than I thought they would. I think everyone's having a great time. How are you doing? Did you find out anything today?"

"I would say that today was very productive. I think we can rule out a couple of people, and although I'm not in law enforcement, I think we're down to two suspects. Here's what I discovered." She related the conversations she'd had with Renee, Antoinette, and Amber, concluding with why she thought Simone and Mac could both be considered viable suspects.

Chief Oliphant was quiet for some time and then he said, "I pretty much agree with everything you've said, but the problem becomes how do we determine which one did it? I don't think either one of them will admit to anything, and although each of them has a motive, we can't put them near the sauna at the time of death. In other words, we can certainly speculate, but we have nothing solid to go on."

"Chief, I made some notes late this afternoon, and I have an idea for a plan that's so off the wall, it might just work. It's kind of a sting operation. I'm thinking if word gets to Mac and Simone that instead of the Serenity Hotel and Spa losing business, it's gone viral, if you will. Judy could say she's even had to hire additional spa personnel because, in addition to the people staying at the hotel, she's also been fully booked with day spa people."

"How do you plan on getting the word out to Mac and Simone?" he asked.

"I was hoping you might have some thoughts on that. Mac should be easy. I can have Judy call him and tell him she has no intention of selling to him or anyone else, since her hotel and spa have been filled to capacity for the next few weeks. I'm not sure how I can let Simone know. Do you have any ideas?"

He was quiet for several minutes and then he said, "My brother-in-law is the editor of the Calistoga News. I'll bet he'd write up an article for it. From what Jim Michaelson told my deputy, we know Simone reads it. We could even have a supposed reporter interview Judy and ask if the problems with the sauna have been fixed, and she can say something like, 'No, the owner of the company that has to fix it is on vacation until Tuesday, but we're being very careful or some such thing like that. When were you thinking about doing something?"

"I think the sooner the better. I'd like to do it tomorrow. I'm a little unclear how I can accomplish the second part. We'll need the parking lot to be filled with cars, because you can't say a hotel and spa are filled to capacity and then there aren't any cars in the lot. I was thinking Judy could rent a bunch of cars for a day, and she and I could drive them here and have her assistant ferry us back to the car rental place."

"I have a better idea. Calistoga's a small town, and I've lived here most of my life. During that time, I've done things for people who, how shall I say it, owe me. One of the people I helped by keeping his son out of the headlines and jail for selling drugs is a car dealer here in town. The agreement was that his son had to prove he'd turned over a new leaf and was no longer involved in any way with drugs. This was several years ago. In return, I told him I wouldn't pursue the case against his son. His father has told me many times how grateful he is that I handled it that way, and he would like to repay the favor by helping me whenever and however he could. This might be the time to collect."

"I don't quite understand what you have in mind, Chief."

"I'll ask him if we could borrow some cars tomorrow, beginning in the morning and keep them at your hotel during the night. He has a bunch of car jockeys that drive the cars wherever they need to be delivered, and they could bring them to you. One of his employees could drive them back to the car lot until they'd delivered all the cars you need. He also has a used car lot, so we could get a number of different kinds of cars. I'll call him and see if that would work for him."

"That would be wonderful."

"If one of the suspects we talked about was to do something, when do you think it would be?" the chief asked.

"I would think in the early evening, when it's dark. Neither one of the suspects would want to be seen around here during the day, and probably the only reason the killer was able to murder Nikki during the day is because he or she figured the spa was so new there wouldn't be many people around. I want to be sure that something gets in the paper about the popularity of the day spa, because it would be Simone's main competition, since there's no hotel attached to La Spa."

"Liz, I think your plan might work. I'll want to have some of my deputies at the hotel and spa when this sting operation of yours goes down. Actually, they could masquerade as guests. Let me make some calls, and I'll get back to you. This needs to be orchestrated very carefully to make it work, but I think we can pull off our part. Let's just hope Mac or Simone cooperates and Liz, even if it doesn't work, you'll know you tried."

"Thanks, Chief. I really want to help my friend Judy, and in order to do that the murderer has to be found, otherwise there's a good chance her hotel and spa, and really her life savings, will be lost."

"As soon as I work out the arrangements, I'll be in touch. Have a good rest of the evening and with a little luck, we might be able to wrap this case up by this time tomorrow. Believe me, with everything else my police force is trying to handle, that would take care of a huge problem for me."

CHAPTER TWENTY-NINE

Liz walked down the hall to the dining room after she ended her call with the chief. Judy had just placed a dish of ice cream in front of where she'd be sitting. "Liz, I bought this from a new ice cream vendor in town. He supposedly makes fresh ice cream every day, and from the tastes I had of different kinds when I visited his shop, it's better than any ice cream I've ever had. I'd like to hear what you think."

Liz took a spoonful and tasted it. She looked over at Judy and said, "I agree. Hands down, this is definitely the best ice cream I've ever had. It's kind of salty with a caramel taste."

"I certainly hope so," Judy said laughing, "because I bought the caramel salt ice cream, and I think his ice cream has just become the benchmark for all the others. It's wonderful. I was thinking of having it available for my guests if they want a late-night snack. What do you think?"

"I think it's a terrific idea, and I'd probably be first in line."

"What did the chief think of your plan?" Judy asked.

"He liked it, and because of all the people he knows in town, he had some great suggestions."

"Like what?"

"Like having his brother-in-law put an article in the local newspaper about how the murder at the hotel has not resulted in any negative publicity, and that the hotel and spa have been fully booked for the coming weeks. He also suggested that there be a blurb in the article about how the actual controls to the sauna can't be fixed until Tuesday, because the man who owns the sauna repair company is on vacation."

"So, you're thinking whatever happens will probably happen tomorrow or tomorrow evening."

"I am."

"What did he think of your idea that I rent cars, and you and I drive them here?"

"He had a better idea. Evidently a few people in this town owe him favors for things he's done in the past for them or their families. One of them owns a car dealership here in town, and he's sure the owner will loan us the cars we need to fill the lot, so it looks like the hotel and spa are successful."

"Liz, it sounds like it might work, but what about the non-existent guests I have here. I mean, we can fill up the parking lot, but if there's nobody in the sauna or the jacuzzi, there's no bait to catch the murderer in the act of doing anything."

"Chief Oliphant is going to have some of his personnel act as guests, so make sure you have plenty of robes, slippers, and towels available."

"That I can do. Actually, I probably should schedule appointments for some of them with my spa personnel, so the whole thing looks like it's authentic."

"You're absolutely right, Judy, I hadn't thought of that. You'll have to pay them, but I think that's an investment you're willing to make in exchange for saving the hotel and spa." She looked down at her purse and said, "My phone's ringing. It must be the chief."

She picked it up and looked at the monitor. "Hi, Chief. That was fast."

"Well, I didn't want to waste time with this. My brother-in-law is going to press shortly with tomorrow's paper, so he'll be calling Mrs. Rasmussen in a few minutes. My friend's car jockeys will start bringing cars to the parking lot at the hotel tomorrow morning around nine. They'll stagger a few more in during the day, so it looks like people are checking in. He even has a couple of female employees who will help, and I have a couple of my deputies doing the same. That way, if anyone is watching, they'll simply see couples and individuals checking into the hotel and for their spa appointments."

"That sounds great. Thank you so much. Do you have anything specifically in mind for the actual sting?" Liz asked.

"What I told my chief deputy, and what he's telling the men and women we'll be using, is that particular attention should be paid to the sauna area since that's where the murder took place. Naturally, we can't have my people in a sauna for several hours at the normal temperature a sauna would be set at, so please have Mrs. Rasmussen keep it lower than usual and provide them with plenty of bottles of water."

"Chief, Judy is calling in some of her spa personnel to provide treatments for your people. Why don't you have your deputy call in the morning, and Judy can match up spa appointments with your people?"

"Will do. Liz, I'm sorry I can't be there, but my people are very well trained, and let's hope for Mrs. Rasmussen's sake, this works. Naturally, I'll be in touch throughout the day and evening. My staff has my number, as do you. Feel free to call me and let's keep our fingers crossed that this works."

"Thanks again, Chief. Let everyone know we'll be here all day, and we'll do everything we can on our end to make this successful. Good night."

She turned to Judy and said, "I know you heard that, so it's definitely a go. I think we need to get a good night's sleep, since it looks like tomorrow may be a very busy day."

Judy reached out and put her hand on Liz's arm. "Thank you for doing this and just being here for me. I never would have come up with a plan like this on my own. If it is Mac or Simone, and at this point I hope it is, I think we, actually the police, stand a very good chance of catching him or her."

"Me, too. Now I need to take Winston out and call Roger. Sleep well."

When she returned to her suite she called Roger. "Hi, Liz. How's my favorite female sleuth doing?"

"Very well, thank you. I just got off the phone with the chief, and we've devised a plan, kind of a sting, that will take place tomorrow." She spent several minutes running it by him. "Roger, do you think I've overlooked anything?"

"No, it sounds pretty thorough. I'm concerned about your safety, but since the police are going to handle it, and I assume you and Judy will be staying in the hotel during the evening, you should be fine. I would like you to keep your gun and Winston with you, even though there will be police on the premises, but strange things can happen. Promise you'll call me tomorrow night and let me know what happens. I'll be thinking about you the whole time. I'd come over and be there with you, but the trial that's starting tomorrow will probably last several days. Be careful, Liz. I love you."

"I love you too, Roger, and Winston says the same. Don't worry, we'll be fine."

CHAPTER THIRTY

When Liz woke up the following morning she looked out the window and thought it was a perfect day to catch a murderer. The sun was shining on the morning dew that had formed on the lawn overnight, creating a fairyland of sparkles.

She took Winston out, fed him, and walked down the hall to the kitchen. "Well, hello, Mary, I didn't expect to see you this morning, since I think I'm the only guest here, unless someone came late last night."

"Mrs. Rasmussen called me last night and asked me to come in. She told me what was planned for today. She wants everything to look like we're completely filled, and she also asked me to make some food for the police and the people from the car dealership. I'd be happy to make you an omelet, if you'd like. Nettie's even here, and she'll bring you some coffee in a minute."

"An omelet sounds wonderful, thanks," Liz said, "I've thought of a few things I want to write down about today, so I'll be in the dining room." She sat down at the big table and made a list of things she and Judy needed to do to ensure that the sting would work. The first thing to be done was to have Judy call Mac and tell him how the hotel and spa had become an overnight hit. Since Mac could see the parking lot from his winery, she wanted Judy to wait until a few of the cars had been delivered.

"Good morning, Liz," Judy said as she came into the dining room and sat down next to her. "I see you're making notes again. Last night I called several of my spa staff members, and I've scheduled a number of appointments with them for the police personnel. If Mac or Simone is watching or has someone watching, I want them to see people going in and out of the spa. I've made sure we have plenty of robes, slippers, and towels. Mary will have food available during the day, actually she's going to make sandwiches and some other things that don't need to be refrigerated. They'll be here in the dining room for anyone who wants them. Other than that, I can't think of anything else, can you?"

"Around eleven or so this morning, I want you to call Mac, but I want you to wait until there are a few cars in the lot, and a few of the police personnel are here. You can thank him for his offers over the months and tell him since you're booked for the next few weeks, there is no way you're going to sell the property. As he's talking to you, say something like, 'I have to go. Two people that don't even have reservations just walked in. Talk to you later, or some such thing.' Say whatever feels natural to you."

Liz looked at the large grandfather clock that stood next to the breakfront cabinet and said, "It's 9:00. Chief Oliphant said they'd start delivering the cars right about now. We should probably get ready for them. The police will begin coming about the same time and continue throughout the day."

They both heard the first car arrive, and a few minutes later the front door of the hotel opened and a male and female police officer registered at the hotel under a false name. It continued throughout the day. Each time one of them registered, Judy told them what kind of a spa appointment she had arranged for them and when it was scheduled. Several times during the day people returned to the office and thanked her, saying it was the best massage or facial or whatever they'd ever had. Judy figured even if they didn't catch the murderer, she was certain the law personnel would help the spa be successful simply by word of mouth.

As the afternoon wore on, Liz became more and more nervous,

hoping her plan would work. At 5:00 that evening, she and Winston went outside and made a loop of the area around the sauna. The lights were on and several law enforcement personnel were in there, but nothing was happening.

She stationed herself at the kitchen window, hoping against hope that she would see something, or that something would take place in the sauna. Everything was quiet. She looked at the trees around the spa and thought she could catch a glimpse of a policemen as he waited for a suspect to make a move.

The time went by excruciatingly slow. Finally, at nine that night Liz had to admit to herself that her plan had failed. There had been absolutely no activity at the spa other than some law enforcement personnel languishing in the jacuzzi or the sauna. The man in charge, Deputy Williams, walked into the hotel and said, "Mrs. Langley, it's late, and I don't think anything is going to happen. There's a city ordinance that spas have to close down at 9:00, and I'm sure both of the suspects know that. I'm going to take my personnel and leave now. I'm really sorry, because it was a very good plan, but it just didn't happen the way we hoped it would."

"Unfortunately, I think you're right. Believe me, I hate to have it end this way, but it is what it is. I guess the only saving grace is that your people were able to have some spa treatments and some great food prepared by Mary. Other than that, it was a wasted day. I'm sure some of your people are going to look like prunes from being in the jacuzzi and sauna too long. On behalf of both Mrs. Rasmussen and me, thank you."

He left, and she walked into to the living room where Judy was silently weeping. "Judy, I am so sorry it didn't work. I really thought it would. We both need a good night's sleep, and we'll think of something else tomorrow. Try not to worry. This was just our first attempt. I need to take Winston out one more time. See you in the morning."

Liz and Winston walked out into the darkness through the kitchen door and back to a grove of trees which separated Judy's property from Mac's. Winston was communing with nature when Liz noticed a movement to her left. Winston lifted his head, instinctively walking silently over to her. She put her hand on his head, indicating he was to be still.

A moment later a shadowy form moved towards the sauna where the police personnel had left the lights on. The mysterious person stopped next to the pile of construction debris, picked up a piece of steel rebar, and then started to fiddle with temperature controls of the sauna.

"Stop," Liz yelled. "Who are you? What are you doing?"

She saw the figure whirl around with a gun in his hand and then he yelled at her. "You're the woman with the dog. You were in my place yesterday, but today you're in the wrong place at the wrong time. Put your hands up, or I'll kill you like I killed that woman in the sauna," the figure said.

"Winston, attack," she whispered to the big ninety-five-pound dog. The dog was faster than the bullet the figure fired at him, as Winston crashed into him, causing the man Liz recognized as Mac Owens to fall to the ground. Simultaneously a voice yelled, "Police, drop the gun and stay where you are."

Liz saw the large figure of Chief Oliphant run over to Mac Owens, who was lying on the ground, and say, "Don't move." He spoke into a small microphone on his lapel and said, "Backup needed. Shots fired. Code three. Serenity Hotel at the sauna."

Liz heard the approaching sirens and said, "Chief, what are you doing here? I thought your vacation didn't end until tomorrow."

"Theoretically it doesn't, but I decided to cut it short. I knew my men had the sauna and jacuzzi covered, but the more I thought about it, the more certain I became that Mac Owens was the murderer. He had the motive, and he also could see Mrs. Rasmussen's property from his wine tasting room. As soon as it got dark I hid in the line of trees that separates his property from the hotel's. When I saw him leave the wine tasting room and begin to walk towards this area, I followed him."

"Thank you," she said as several police officers ran towards Mac and the chief.

"You can call your dog off now that my men are here." He turned to his deputy, motioned towards Mac Owens, and said, "Take him to the station and book him for the murder of Nikki Evans. I have his confession on tape as well as a witness, Mrs. Langley."

Just then a car raced into the parking lot. A man threw the door open and ran back to where Liz, the chief, his men, and Mac were. It was Roger.

"Roger, what are you doing here?" Liz asked.

"The chief called and was concerned you might try to get involved in the sting instead of staying in the house. He asked if I could drive over here and keep an eye on you to make sure you didn't get into any trouble. I planned on being here about two hours ago, but there was a horrible accident on the freeway and I had to just sit there waiting for the Highway Patrol to open the lanes, getting more and more nervous as the minutes ticked by. Are you okay?" he asked as he pulled her to him and patted Winston on the head.

"I'm fine. Oh, Roger, I was so sure my sting idea wasn't going to work, and Judy was going to lose everything. Thank heavens it did, although I'm not too sure what would have happened if it hadn't been for Winston and the chief."

Roger pushed her away at arm's length and said, "Where's the pistol I gave you? The one you promised me you'd have with you at all times."

"I did, Roger. It was with me all day, but when all the police left, and we were sure the sting wasn't going to work, I left it inside while I went out to walk Winston. We were all sure that the murderer was a no-show, so I didn't think it was necessary."

"Liz, it was necessary. Please, please, promise me if you're ever again involved with anything else like this you'll have a gun with you every minute, although it would be just fine with me if this was the last time."

"Roger, if it's any consolation, it would be just fine with me as well. I need to go tell Judy what's happened. I'm sure she heard the sirens, and she's probably a nervous wreck about now."

"Go on in. I'll be there in a few minutes. I want to talk to the chief. Winston, go with Liz."

Liz and Winston walked back into the hotel where Judy was anxiously looking out through one of the windows. "Judy, it's over. It was Mac, and the chief's men are taking him to the police station and booking him for Nikki's murder. I'm sure the paper will run a story on it tomorrow, and the Serenity Hotel and Spa will be cleared in full."

Judy started to cry. "I can't thank you enough, Liz. I was sure when we didn't think the plan had worked that my time as a spa owner and hotelier had been very short-lived. I was actually ready to call Mac and take whatever offer he wanted to give me, so I could salvage something from it. Now there's a good chance the hotel and spa really will be successful, and I owe it all to you."

"You don't need to think that the hotel and spa are going to be successful, Judy. I think the operative words are that they will be successful, and it couldn't happen to a more deserving person. Now, if you want to thank me, you could book a massage for me the next time I come. I'd love to have one tomorrow, but Roger drove over, and since he's involved in a trial, we need to drive back tonight, but first he needs to switch cars with you."

She and Winston walked back to their suite. She packed in a matter of minutes and when Roger walked in she said, "I'm ready to go. If we leave now, we'll make it back just in time to see Brandy Boy deliver his last nip of brandy for the night to my guests at the Red Cedar Lodge."

MURDER IN CALISTOGA

RECIPES

JUDY'S PHEASANT

Ingredients:
2 pheasants
½ cup flour + 2 tbsp. flour
4 tbsp. cooking oil
½ cup sliced mushrooms (I prefer fresh ones to canned.)
1 can mushroom soup
½ cup half and half
½ cup white wine
2 tbsp. chopped parsley for garnish

Directions:
Preheat oven to 325 degrees. Cut the legs and breasts from pheasants and discard the rest. Heat oil in frying pan over medium high heat. Dredge the pheasant breasts and legs in ½ cup flour. Place the pieces in the frying pan and brown all sides for about five minutes. Remove from the pan and dry on paper towels. Place the pheasant pieces in a 9 x 13-inch ovenproof pan.

Drain all but 2 tablespoons of oil from the frying pan. Add 2 tablespoons flour, soup, half and half, wine, and mushrooms to the pan and cook over low heat until blended. Pour the mixture over the pheasant pieces, cover with tin foil, and bake for 1 ¼ hours. Remove from the oven and garnish with parsley. Enjoy!

NOTE: Great served over noodles or rice.

CANTALOUPE MOUSSE

Ingredients:
1 ripe cantaloupe
¼ cup heavy cream
2 tbsp. granulated sugar
1 tbsp. apricot brandy or other fruit liqueur (optional)

Directions:
Cut off the top third of the cantaloupe and remove the seeds. Scoop ten or so balls out of the cantaloupe with a melon ball cutter and reserve them. With a spoon, remove the rest of the pulp from inside the cantaloupe leaving the melon shell.

Puree the pulp in a blender with the cream, sugar, and brandy. Pour the mixture into a small bowl and freeze for 30 minutes. Stir the mousse and freeze for an additional ten minutes. Transfer the mixture to the melon shell and freeze it for ten minutes. Top the mousse with the reserved melon balls and sprinkle them with the brandy. Enjoy!

MINI HAM AND EGG CASSEROLES

Ingredients:
¼ of a baguette, cut into small cubes (I've used croutons in place of baguette cubes and it worked great)
4 oz. cream cheese, cut crosswise into 12 pieces (This is super cook friendly. If you have some cheese you want to use up, you can certainly substitute it.)
1 tbsp. extra virgin olive oil + additional for drizzling

¼ lb. ham, chopped (about one cup) (I see no reason why any meat, or for that matter, shrimp, etc. couldn't be used.)
4 scallions, both white and green parts
1 tbsp. freshly ground pepper
1 ½ cups half and half
6 large eggs (I usually use jumbo)
1 tsp. fresh thyme leaves
Spray oil

Directions:
Preheat the oven to 350 degrees. Grease a muffin or mini-muffin pan with the spray oil. Fill each cup halfway with baguette cubes. Top each with a cream cheese piece. In a small frying pan, heat the olive oil and add the ham, white pieces of the scallions, and a pinch of pepper. Cook, stirring until the scallions are tender, about 5 minutes. Stir in the half and half and bring to a simmer. Remove from the heat.

In a medium bowl whisk eggs and thyme together. When they're mixed add the half and half mixture and pour the combined mixture over the baguette cubes. Bake in the oven until puffed and golden brown around the edges, about 15 minutes. Let rest for 5 minutes. Run a knife around the edges and invert onto a baking rack. Sprinkle with the green part of the onions. Enjoy!

NOTE: I like to make these as an appetizer in mini-muffin pans. Watch to make sure they don't burn, but I've found they usually take a little longer than the suggested 15-minute baking time. If you're using a muffin pan, up the time to about 25 minutes.

CLAM CHOWDER IN BREAD BOWLS

Ingredients:
8 slices bacon, diced
1 cup chopped green onions
½ brown onion, chopped

4 medium sized potatoes, peeled and cut into ½ inch cubes
1 stalk celery, thinly sliced
2 medium sized carrots, thinly sliced
1 clove garlic, minced
2 cups water
1 tsp. sea salt (You can use table salt.)
½ tsp. white pepper (If you don't have white, use freshly ground black pepper.)
1 tsp. Worcestershire
8 drops liquid hot pepper sauce such as Tabasco
2 cans evaporated milk
4-5 cans whole baby clams
2 cups half and half
2 bottles clam juice (I use these to thin the soup if it needs it. Totally a matter of personal preference.)
4 – 6 large round sourdough bread rolls

Directions:
On the top of the bread, make an incision about 2 inches in from the edge and cut out a piece (think of it as a lid to your bread bowl.) Remove the lid and set aside. Scoop out most of the bread with a large fork. You can discard it or use it to make homemade croutons, which is what I do. Set aside.

In a large deep pan cook the bacon over medium heat until crisp. Add onions, potatoes, celery, carrots, garlic, water, salt, pepper, Worcestershire, hot pepper sauce, and evaporated milk. Bring to a boil and reduce heat. Cover and simmer until the potatoes are tender, about 15 minutes. Add the clams and the half and half. Heat until steaming, but not boiling. Ladle into the bread bowls, cover with the bread lids, and serve. Enjoy!

BANANA AND NUT MUFFINS

Ingredients:
3 large bananas, mashed
¾ cup white sugar

1 egg
1/3 cup butter, melted
1 ½ cups all-purpose flour
1 tsp baking powder
½ tsp. salt
½ cup walnut pieces
Non-stick spray or paper liners

Directions:
Preheat oven to 350 degrees. Coat muffin pans with non-stick spray, or use paper liners. Sift together the flour, baking powder, baking soda, and salt. Set aside. Combine bananas, sugar, egg, and melted butter. Fold in flour mixture and mix until smooth. Gently stir in the walnuts. Scoop into muffin pan.

Bake in preheated oven. Bake mini-muffins for 10 to 15 minutes, and large muffins for 25 – 30 minutes. When the muffins spring back when lightly tapped, remove them from the oven. Serve and enjoy!

Paperbacks & Ebooks for FREE

Go to www.dianneharman.com/freepaperback.html and get your FREE copies of Dianne's books and favorite recipes immediately by signing up for her newsletter.

Once you've signed up for her newsletter you're eligible to win three paperbacks. One lucky winner is picked every week. Hurry before the offer ends!

ABOUT THE AUTHOR

Dianne lives in Huntington Beach, California, with her husband, Tom, a former California State Senator, and her boxer dog, Kelly. Her passions are cooking, reading, and dogs, so whenever she has a little free time, you can either find her in the kitchen, playing with Kelly in the back yard, or curled up with the latest book she's reading.

Her award winning books include:

Midlife Journey Series
Alexis

Cedar Bay Cozy Mystery Series
Kelly's Koffee Shop, Murder at Jade Cove, White Cloud Retreat, Marriage and Murder, Murder in the Pearl District, Murder in Calico Gold, Murder at the Cooking School, Murder in Cuba, Trouble at the Kennel, Murder on the East Coast, Trouble at the Animal Shelter

Liz Lucas Cozy Mystery Series
Murder in Cottage #6, Murder & Brandy Boy, The Death Card, Murder at The Bed & Breakfast, The Blue Butterfly, Murder at the Big T Lodge

High Desert Cozy Mystery Series
Murder & The Monkey Band, Murder & The Secret Cave, Murdered by Country Music, Murder at the Polo Club

Midwest Cozy Mystery Series
Murdered by Words, Murder at the Clinic

Jack Trout Cozy Mystery Series
Murdered in Argentina

Coyote Series
Blue Coyote Motel, Coyote in Provence, Cornered Coyote

Website: www.dianneharman.com
Blog: www.dianneharman.com/blog
Email: dianne@dianneharman.com

Newsletter

If you would like to be notified of her latest releases please go to www.dianneharman.com and sign up for her newsletter.

Made in the USA
Coppell, TX
05 July 2021